The **Honeylicker** Angel

The **Honeylicker** Angel

ANNA ELKINS

w o r d b o d y

Second Edition: 2017

w o r d b o d y
PO Box 509
Jacksonville, OR 97530

Cover design by Anna Elkins

ISBN-13: 978-0615781945
ISBN-10: 0615781942

Printed in the USA

For all the Melissas, whatever your names may be.

CONTENTS

Life is a flower for which love is the honey.
—Victor Hugo

PROLOGUE

My name is Melissa.

For most of my life, I thought my name was simply what I was called. But I have discovered that it is also my calling. Every time you say my name, you speak my destiny.

Melissa.

PART ONE

Once upon a time, not long ago, in France . . .

CHAPTER 1

When the train slowed into Marseille, a bee hit my window with enough force that I could hear it through the glass. I had been brinking on sleep, and the sound, matched with the almost motionless stop, made me feel that I was not waking but just beginning to dream.

The woman across from me smiled and rose. The other passengers began pulling down their bags from the overhead racks. I didn't bother looking for mine. It wasn't there.

I slung my purse over one shoulder and held my backpack close as I would in a Chicago crowd. In the press of exit, I stepped down to the platform and away from the train. Only then did I notice I had been holding my breath. I let it out and inhaled the scent of trash-trodden cement in warm sunlight. Instead of gray skies, a bright blue heaven opened above me shot with quick, white clouds. I stood on my toes, looking for my aunt's head—which usually meant looking for a large hat in full plumage. I saw plenty of hats but no Tifi.

Around me pulsed French laughter, welcomes, hollers, exclamations. The station was vibrant and tight with arrivals; you could have crowd-surfed across us. In the swirling sea of people, I stood still, watching lovers kiss, feeling the elbows of mothers hugging children. I stood until the crowds thinned from the platform and filled the station body, and I was left alone with the breeze and the ticket stubs it sent spinning.

I bit my lip and winced. Days later, and it still smarted.

This was a mistake. All of it was a mistake but especially thinking Aunt Tifi's gift was a sign.

Where was she? I finally started walking toward the front of the train which had pulled deep into the terminus under a domed glass ceiling. I glanced behind me where the end of the train lay far out along the rails, gleaming. I sighed and walked away from it, the only familiar thing I knew in this place.

Under the glass ceiling, everyone's head was aglow in warm but distant light. I kept looking for a certain Cheshire grin heralded by clanging bangles. I saw dark men in pale robes and small children with large, square school packs. They all filtered in and out of the wall of doors lining the station entrance. I followed a woman wearing heels to one of the doors. She walked through, and I stopped on the threshold. Before me, a great precipice of steps descended into the city. A man bumped into me from behind, and I stepped aside to let him out before returning inside.

I walked to a bank of chairs. A little boy bounced by with a yellow balloon tied to one wrist, his mother holding him by the other. I sat down and watched them leave.

My aunt was lovable if not exactly reliable. She always had a reasonable explanation for missing concerts, forgetting to buy groceries, losing keys. When I was ten, my mother and I had visited her in North Carolina. After mom got sick from Aunt Tifi's attempt at *boeuf bourguignon,* Aunt Tifi apologized by taking me to the State Fair. She bought me a cloud of cotton candy and told me to meet her at the dart throwing booth in fifteen minutes. A nice security guard brought my limping aunt to me over an hour later. She had caught her skirts in the Ferris Wheel gears after convincing the operator to explain the mechanics to her. Her ankle had twisted when she tried to extricate herself. I had passed part of my time sitting with SERAPHINA! ORACLE OF YOUR FUTURE!! who told me I would find true love, have four children, and live to a grand old age after various trials.

When I had relayed this to my aunt, she frowned. "Stuff and nonsense. Here, let me lean on you. Ouch, that's better. Be careful who you listen to about your future."

"But I thought you liked fortune telling, Aunt Tifi."

She laughed and adjusted her enormous star pendant. "I suppose that's a fair mistake. I prefer to ask for signs."

"Ask who?"

We were interrupted by a clown carrying a bouquet of balloons so big it blocked the sky. Aunt Tifi bought a dozen balloons for me, and I forgot about signs.

I wanted one now—a sign, that is. I stood up, stiff, and looked around for the information desk. A row of croissants was distracting me when a lanky man in black came through a side door at a brisk pace, carrying a piece of cardboard at knee level. He brushed passed me saying *"Pardon,"* before starting forward again.

"No problem," I told his retreating back, readjusting my purse and wondering about pick-pockets. Mid-stride, he stopped and turned back toward me, holding up an eyebrow and the board. The name "Melissa" was scrawled across it in thin, black letters. My name.

I looked at it for several seconds before pointing to the letters. "What is that?"

He stuck his neck and the board forward. "A sign. You are Melissa? I am your cousin, Blaise. Come, we are late. We talk in the car." He turned on his heel through the door he had entered.

"*We* are late? Wait a minute, where is my Aunt Tifi?"

He turned and looked at me, "She tell me to pick you up. So I am here. *Voilà.* Come."

"But. . . ." I protested to his back. He was already out the door before I moved to follow him. He was plowing past cars and busses toward a dented Renault truck parked at an angle, half on the sidewalk.

Blaise was already pulling open the driver's door before he asked, "Your bag. You have baggage?"

"It was lost in Paris." I pulled my backpack around to my chest. "Or Chicago."

"Oh. We go then." He got in and slammed his door. I didn't move. My head throbbed and my teeth felt furry. I wanted a clean, bright taxi and a skyline with the Sears Tower. But Blaise had already started to back the truck away. With a hand holding a cigarette, he made small, fast circles at me through the windshield. "Quick."

I took a deep breath. The air was a cross between public dumpster and honey. A woman walked by in a bright, shabby sun dress, the afternoon light casting her shadow across mine. I shut my eyes, opened them and opened the passenger door. I had to heave it three times before it yielded. Blaise was already a car length away before I had closed it. He was filling the interior of the cab with smoke and French music.

I poked between the seat cushions for a buckle. Blaise's cell phone rang, and he dug in his jacket pocket. He found what he was looking for, I didn't. I let the belt feed back, but it hung slack and banged against my arm every time he braked. I remembered, with no energy for regret, that I had forgotten my cell phone. It was sitting on my kitchen counter back home.

Blaise started a loud phone discussion, swerved out into traffic, and began speeding down narrow streets. I briefly wondered if my health insurance policy was valid overseas.

Blaise drove, spoke on his phone, and used his cigarette as a pointer. To the phone, he gestured with a fall of ash, "My brother, *merde!*" To the large church on a hill, he crossed himself with even more ash: "There is our big lady cathedral." I imagined the view from there to here, all us of tiny and anonymous.

We had turned onto a wide boulevard that gently descended toward a port. The Sea—my first glimpse of the Mediterranean. I expected it to look like Lake Michigan, but the light resting on the water was full and cloying, washing the port's buildings in an orange glow. I found myself with palms pressed to the window that wouldn't roll down, thinking of an afternoon sipping a *café au lait* by the water.

Within seconds, the church disappeared, the Sea disappeared. The Renault took tiny streets away from *café*s and shops, and I was left with a neighborhood of shadows and barred windows. I sank back onto the plastic seat and waited for this distant cousin of mine to finish his phone call and tell me what had happened to my aunt.

CHAPTER 2

Blaise was my cousin by marriage. Aunt Tifi married his uncle, Jean-Luc, when she was an airline stewardess in the Sixties. That was back before political correctness and flight attendants. The Frenchman and the American fell in love and moved to North Carolina where Uncle Jean-Luc taught his native language at the university, and Aunt Tifi studied gardening. She could keep anything alive that grew in the earth, but not my uncle. He needed more than good soil and love. He died of a heart attack when I was in college.

"His heart was just too dang big," Tifi had said, sniffing.

In his will, Uncle Jean-Luc had requested that Tifi scatter his ashes in his homeland. She complied, horrifying the French relatives with the thought of cremation.

I had only met one member of Uncle Jean-Luc's family before today: Blaise's brother. He had visited my aunt and uncle in Greensboro a couple of years after the State Fair trip. Aunt Tifi had invited me to come and meet him that summer, thinking I'd enjoy getting to know a cousin. Instead, I spent a week annoyed at a gangly, mischievous teenager who spiked my hot chocolate with enough chili powder that my throat felt like a burning building. I tried to remember his name.

And now I was in a car with his brother whose manners didn't seem to be much better. Blaise came to a full stop on a steep street. He yanked the parking brake high, leaving the truck facing uphill at a thirty-degree angle. He scrambled out the door before the truck had shaken to a stop, crossed the thin street, and stepped over the tiny sidewalk directly onto a peeling door stoop. He pushed a button near a series of mail slots. Some looked residential, others boasted business logos. He inhaled the last of his tobacco and let the butt fall, crushing it between his heel and a flattened aluminum can. The door opened, and he disappeared inside with a slam.

I craned my neck to look up at the buildings. Their façades faced each other like long-warring neighbors leaning at weary attention, wearing weathered uniforms of chipped paint and amulets of laundry lines fluttering their colors in the breeze. French doors pressed against balconies that didn't appear wide enough to stand on. A woman, four floors up on my side of the street, stood inside her room resting elbows out on the railing. She watched me, the car. Her hair lifted from her solid face in the breeze.

I heard voices. Blaise and another man appeared then disappeared behind the truck. The back door opened. The truck rocked with the weight of someone crawling inside.

Shuffle. Pause. Slam.

The other man returned to his door with a box and nodded.

Blaise held up his hand in a stationary wave. He yanked his door open, sat squarely on his seat, clapped his hands, and smiled, dialing a number on his phone. "We go now. The last delivery."

Before I could ask what he had delivered, Blaise had already started the motor and another phone conversation. We lurched up the hill, accelerated to its crest, and descended. I lost all semblance of direction. I could only wonder which way the Sea lay, a turquoise stranger I wanted to know.

I was starting to get carsick. I tried to focus on the road, but Blaise drove like even the road was an obstacle. He ended a call and tossed his phone on the dashboard. "So, Tifi. Where is she?"

For a second, I wondered if I had asked the question. My head felt like a throbbing cotton ball. "That's what I'd like to know. Last I heard, she was galloping across Tunisia. We were going to meet here in Marseille."

Blaise shrugged. "She sends telegram to my parents

yesterday. They tell me she is delay in *Tunis*. Can't come. I have deliveries, so I come."

"Did she say when she planned on arriving?" Even as I asked, I remembered Aunt Tifi had a loose definition of the word "plan."

"Soon. She wants to come and taste my new *hydromel*." He tilted his head and slouched back. "It tastes like sunlight on the lips of a woman you have just kissed."

I blinked. Where had that come from? I looked at Blaise in surprise and realized I had expected such words from Frenchmen—not the brusque monotone I'd heard since he had picked me up at the station. He seemed to have some romance in him after all.

He went on, *"Hydromel*—mead, you call it—is the oldest alcohol drink on earth. Before man used grapes, he used honey."

The romance waned. I didn't like honey.

He continued, "The people *préhistorique*, they see honey fall from hives. It falls down. Rain falls down. The rain leaves pools for the honey to swim in. Wild yeasts grow and *voilà*—mead. You may think it is too sweet this mead but no. There are so many kinds."

I was trying not to think of the bees that were the prerequisite for honey. I was even less a fan of bees than of their byproduct.

The traffic seemed to disappear to Blaise as he used his umpteenth cigarette to illustrate the height of *tout les fleurs* in open pastures. "And I want to renovate the old mill. Turn it into factory for the *hydromel*. Then we can sell it all in France. Maybe even in your America. But Chance. . . ."

He stopped and frowned, flicking ash across the gear shift. I wondered if he was about to begin a soliloquy on fate. Then I remembered.

"Chance. That's your brother name, isn't it?"

Blaise focused on the rear-view mirror for a moment before replying. *"La voix du sang est la plus forte.* The voice of blood is the strongest. *Hmmph."*

"We have a similar saying: 'Blood is thicker than water.'"

Blaise laughed without smiling. "Not thicker than honey."

Someone honked, interrupting brotherly tensions.

"Looks like rush hour back home," I said as Blaise brought the truck within inches of the bumper in front of us, trying to merge onto the *autoroute.*

"Rush hour? Yes, everyone going home. Here we call it *bouchon.* It is the word for the cork in a bottle."

"In Chicago 'the cork' is awful. I'm usually in the car two hours a day."

Blaise looked at me. My armpits felt sticky, and I wanted to change my socks. He looked incredulous. "Every day you do this? *Mais non.* That is crazy. I am hating this driving into the city. I come every few months. From the Languedoc. I go enough crazy doing this," he spread his hand out at the jammed cars. As if he had waved a wand, they started moving.

"Have you always worked for your family?"

"Yes, in many things. Both my brother and me.

But now he wants to cook and I want to make *hydromel.*" He shrugged, "My parents' work is not so hard."

"What kind of. . . ." The Renault and my question squealed to a halt, and Blaise started yelling in French through the windshield. That not sufficient, he rolled his window down in heaving yanks and bolted his torso out of it, hollering at the driver ahead. His leather jacket stretched and sagged in time with his gesticulations. He landed back in his seat with a tight sigh. His cell phone rang, and he started yet another animated discussion, occasionally banging on the horn. This seemed more for conversational emphasis since, once again, no one ahead of or behind us was moving.

As soon as he finished his call, Blaise cranked on the radio to full volume. Conversation seemed officially over. Most of the songs were American. At every unintelligible commercial break, I marveled that I was in France.

I leaned my head against the back of my seat and imagined arriving to a gracious Provence cottage. There would be ivy around windows hung with white curtains. There would be polished bed frames with fluffy, down comforters enveloped in hand-quilted duvets. Maybe the cottage was built into the picturesque mill Blaise had mentioned.

We left the *autoroute* and began heading toward the setting sun. Fields rolled, golden and soft in all directions. Off and on, we paralleled a thin canal lined with great, leafy plane trees. It seemed to follow us. The gentle green of its water lay placid, the banks just wide enough apart for two boats to pass each other. I'd have to try a boat while I was here.

This was the kind of countryside I'd seen in movies and guidebooks. Crumbly manses, spired churches with clock towers, farmers in dark hats. And so I was shocked at each neon sign attached to a medieval building and at box stores on the outskirts of villages that could have been the sets for an historic film—a film without the pulsating rock music, perhaps. Blaise was tapping his fingers on the steering wheel in time to The Rolling Stones.

Outside, the land was a Ravel composition. The canal appeared again to our left, and the shade from its trees enveloped the Renault. When the road veered away from the water again, it passed through open vineyards.

One half of the sky was filling with clouds. The other half was clear. Divided like the sky, I only half wanted to return home.

It was dark and starting to rain by the time Blaise pulled off the road and descended a drive into a courtyard. The windshield was stippled with water.

He pulled the truck to a stop. "We are here."

I had just enough time to notice we were parked in a clearing alongside the canal before the headlights flicked off.

The dark was sudden as spilled ink. I looked for lights. "Where is the house?"

Blaise was halfway out of the truck. "House? My parents live on a *péniche.*"

I leaned forward to look, and the springs of my seat squeaked. As my eyes adjusted, the length of what must be a barge began to take shape behind the wet glass. A soft glow of colors refracted through the beading rain. Tapping sounded on my window. Blaise. He opened my door and tried to light a cigarette.

I climbed out, holding a hand over my face to keep the rain off. Even in the dark, I could tell the barge was a regal old vessel. The colors—green, gold, and violet—came from a stained-glass window over the wheelhouse door. I could barely make out stacks of small crates crammed onto the prow.

The sharp smell of tobacco cut through the rain. "You speak no French, so I teach you a word: *péniche.*" He pointed at the barge. "It is build in the 1920s. In Germany. It was my grandfather's. He was German, too."

"That's nice. Can we go inside the *péniche?* It's a bit wet out here." I shivered and Blaise answered by walking around the truck.

He took a drag on his cigarette and then left it in his mouth as he tapped on the back doors. "First I take things out. You can maybe help me carry?"

"Of course." I felt oddly honored. Blaise struck me as the sort of man who didn't like to ask for help.

He left his cigarette in his mouth, yanked the doors

open one at a time, and reached for a box. There was that fragrance from Marseille, a slight whiff of . . . oh no.

I looked closer then recoiled. Oh yes.

My head filled with a droning hum. My legs seemed to disappear. I don't remember hitting the ground.

PART TWO

Chicago, Illinois. One week earlier . . .

CHAPTER 3

If my mother had not named me Melissa.

If Aunt Tifi hadn't sent me the borage for my birthday.

If my car had started that morning.

That morning.

My alarm clock pierced the day awake. I did not hear it as sound but instead tasted it as the flavor of lemon. Not the preserved lemon juice I bought in yellow plastic bottles. *Lemon.* In its dimpled skin, its bright, bitter pulp. The sound of my alarm had turned to lemon.

This so surprised me that I lay back in bed to think about it and slept in.

The sun woke me an hour later. Late! I kicked off my sheets and jumped into my clothes. I ran down the stairs of my apartment building pulling on a sweater. But the morning was warm and muggy, so I ran toward my car pulling the sweater off. With one elbow stuck in a sleeve, I took a shortcut across a long planter. I tripped and landed, tangled, on wet mulch. Too late to think of changing, I reached my car and started it. Or, I tried to start it. The old hatchback made wheezing attempts to turn over and then, as if mimicking me, it went back to sleep.

I sat still while tension clamped my body to the seat. I looked across my muddied leg to the keys swinging from the ignition. It was my turn to bring a dozen donuts to the Monday-morning office meeting.

By the time the keys stopped moving, I wondered if I liked donuts. In fact, I wondered if I liked my job. I decided I didn't have the energy to wonder whether or not I liked my life. I shouldered open the door, climbed out, and slammed it shut. I walked back toward my building and climbed up the stairs. At the top, I paused. I looked back, sensing I had dropped or forgotten something. The only things visible were my wet tracks, one side muddier than the other.

For a second, I remembered a time when my feet had been bare and half as large. I had run from the sprinkler into the house, delighted to look back at the evidence of myself, delighted that my footsteps had run to catch up with me.

These days, delight was distant as the moon.

Back inside my apartment, I set my purse in the entryway and headed for the phone. I dialed the office. Elliot would scold. *Ri-i-i-ing.* Then he'd greet me tomorrow with twice the pile of spreadsheets. *Ri-i*—I hung up. How many years had it been since I'd taken a sick day?

I changed out of my muddy clothes, leaving them in a heap on the floor. Back in my paisley pajamas, I leaned on the arm of the couch, my single piece of living room furniture.

Had I already lived here a year? So much for the upgrade apartment. I'd been so busy that I'd never fully unpacked to enjoy it. A box of college books sat in the corner, the packing tape starting to curl away from the cardboard. A commemorative wine glass gathered dust in the window. On top of the television sat the one picture I'd bothered to frame. It was taken in France. Afternoon light struck Aunt Tifi's face in a flattering way, softening her stark features as she kissed my Uncle Jean-Luc. It was the kind of picture I would love to be in.

I had a vague craving for a croissant.

In the kitchen, my cupboards were filled with boxes: cold cereal, hot cereal, pancake mix, waffle mix. Even the fridge: boxes of fat-free lunch meats, cartons of skim milk and egg substitute. Did everything come in a box, or had I not been paying attention? I looked for something unsquare and noticed a little bottle of lemon juice. I unscrewed the green cap and sniffed it. It landed in the trash.

I microwaved fake eggs with bits of pre-sliced ham and took my meal back to the couch. Instead of the news, I flipped to cartoons.

Cartoons turned to soaps and soaps to talk shows.

Someone knocked on my door as Oprah

introduced a financial guru. I turned off the TV, slipped off the couch into my slippers, and headed toward the entryway. Through the peep hole, I saw a blur of brown resembling a delivery man with a package instead of a head. I pulled back the chain and opened the door. To the package, I said, "Hi?"

A face materialized on one side of the wrappings. It looked relieved. The man started speaking without discernible sentence breaks. "Oh good I didn't want to have to drag this back to the truck Nice neighborhood here Should I set it inside for you?"

I held the door open. "Thanks. Is it heavy?"

He shuffled in, setting the thing down with a solid thud where an area rug should be. The package looked like someone had tried to wrap a three-foot topiary in paper bags.

"I think it's a plant Yep it says plant." Rolf, according to his name tag, had consulted his computerized tablet.

"From?" I peered down at the address. "Aunt Tifi!" I said, crouching down and starting to pull off the paper.

"Would you mind signing for it?" asked Rolf. "And there's a letter too It was taped to the package but it came off so you. . . ."

I wasn't listening. I was thinking of my aunt billowing about in a muumuu, deadheading roses and singing "Beyond the Sea" with Bobby Darin on LP from the screened-in porch.

Pulling away several layers of paper, I revealed a

plastic globe, stabilized at the bottom by a couple of books. Curious, I lifted off the plastic to find a cluster of blue, star-shaped flowers. The stems were furry, the leaves dark.

I touched a petal and leaned forward to smell it. Before I could detect a fragrance, a bee shot from the heart of a star and stung me on my lower lip.

CHAPTER 4

Rolf was still waiting for me to sign, his own lower lip sticking out. "Did a bee just sting you?"

I covered my mouth with my hand. I was still crouching before the partially exposed mystery plant, shaking my head. This hadn't happened. *No, no, no. I hate bees. I'm sure I'm allergic. . . .*

He leaned closer. "But I thought I saw. . . ."

"Yeth. It thung me." I stood up too fast and felt lightheaded. I leaned against the wall and closed my eyes. "How did it get in there?"

"You OK?"

I took my hand away from my lip, and Rolf leaned forward. "I think it's swelling Maybe you're allergic My brother's gotta carry around one of those EpiPens all the time or he'll die You know you can die from a bee sting?"

I could feel my heart beat in the wall behind me. "I've been thung before, when I was little." A deep memory surfaced like a bubble on still water. It popped. "I have an EpiPen thumwhere."

He shook his head. "Doesn't matter Sometimes your first sting no problem But later watch out Peter my brother he has to jab adrenaline in his. . . ."

I crushed my palms to my ears. My head started spinning, and I tried to take a complete breath. I hated bees. I hated that the one day I missed work, this delivery man had come to my door. If I hadn't answered the door, I could have learned something useful on Oprah, like how to buy a house and pay it off before I die.

Rolf was still talking, ". . . and he gets hives and swells up like a balloon. . . ."

I slid down the wall trying to take in air.

Rolf's voice turned to the bright zest of lemon.

Nurses in scrubs. Glaring lights. Corridors. Rolf announcing "Special delivery" to the emergency room where he drove me. Between hyperventilating and hives, I remember being thankful I lived a few blocks from the hospital.

Eventually I found myself lying on a bed—still in my pajamas—while a woman in scrubs and a white jacket took my blood pressure. I opened and closed my mouth. When I reached up to touch my lower lip, it felt swollen but not awful.

The woman glanced at me and back at a gauge.

"Ah, we're awake. How do we feel?"

"Shaky."

She leaned in to look at my lip and snapped back to standing, every movement a whirl of hurry. "I'm Dr. Corago. You'll be fine. Convenient that the delivery man was there when you were stung. That reminds me." She pulled a folded, oversized pink envelope from her pocket. "He left a letter for you. Said it came with the plant." She handed the envelope to me.

I reached for it, noticing an ID bracelet around my wrist. I held the letter blankly in front of me. "Thank you."

She tilted her head in practice instead of compassion and asked, "Have you been stung by bees before?"

"Once and badly when I was very young." I shivered. "I think I'm allergic to them."

Dr. Corago's pager beeped. She checked it saying, "Doubt it. You're more likely to die in a car accident on the way to the hospital than to die of anaphylaxis. We can run a test if you'd like." She clipped her pager back on her belt, poised to depart. "But I'll wager you almost died because you were afraid you would." She looked at me for two full seconds. "It's strange, did you know *Melissaphobia* is fear of bees? Your name means 'honey bee' in Greek." She gave a short laugh that didn't reach her eyes. "Maybe you should make peace with them."

She patted her pager. "Have to run." And with that, she turned on her heel and left me with humiliation and the envelope. I decided to focus on the latter.

The return address was as familiar as my own. Aunt Tifi wrote me every spring and fall, "When I put the seeds in and when I pull the flowers out."

The last time I had been to her house in Greensboro we had spent a weekend watching black-and-white Jimmy Stewart films. Stewart reminded Aunt Tifi of Uncle Jean-Luc. We had sat on her red couch sipping hot cocoa with inches of hand-whipped cream while the white Angora, Shirley Temple of Doom, shed her winter coat. By the time I left, the couch looked more pink than red.

Pink. I ripped open the envelope. It was like opening another era, one with a whiff of jasmine, monogrammed stationery, and spidery longhand.

My dearest Melissa,

I hope it arrived safely. I've been growing it in my sunroom over the winter. Have you ever heard of borage? (bourragé *in French). In English, it's a lousy name for a lovely flower. Herb, really. Nicer to call it "star flower." It has another colloquial name, but I can't recall it at the moment. That's one of the mixed beauties of advancing age, love: forgetfulness. It's good when you don't want to remember something but bad when you do.*

Anyway, I thought you could use a little color after a long, mid-western winter. As always, things are warm already here in Greensboro, though we did have a marvelous ice storm that made all the trees look like they'd been dipped in crystal. You should've seen it! I lost a large limb over the porch. Smashed through the sunroom and flattened all of my flowers. As I was cleaning up the debris, I found this one star flower, knocked out of its planter but half alive. I had been thinking of you all morning and was wondering what to send you. So do forgive the late gift (I've been nursing it back to health) and. . . .

Happiest belated birthday! To celebrate, I want you to come to France and meet Jean-Luc's family. I won't take no for an answer this time, planes or no planes. You haven't taken a proper vacation in years—life is short! Enjoy it!

Ticket enclosed (I hope I get this in the mail in time). I am expecting you.

Yours,

Aunt Tifi

In different ink, at the bottom of the page:

P.S. Change in plans. Can't meet you in Paris. I'll be traveling from Morocco to Tunisia. Catch a train to Marseille when you arrive. Will meet you there.

P.P.S. Try the borage leaves in a cocktail (looks great in gin on the rocks). Good for stress, too—the plant itself, I mean. Though maybe best in combination with *the gin.*

And written up the side of the letter:

P.P.P.S. "Beebread." That's the other name for the borage.

I swallowed, glad my throat no longer felt swollen. I looked at ticket and the tiny dash between Chicago and Paris. As if there were no distance, no large metal plane, no ocean between them.

The ticket date was for the day after tomorrow.

My first thought was a type-A's frustration with impetuosity. Leave in two days? Ridiculous. Impossible. Elliot would never let me off work on such short notice.

My second thought was: *I am pathetic.* I was nearing thirty, I'd never been on a plane, and I didn't like my job. Maybe I even hated it. Yet I was afraid of giving up the security that came with it, even if that security meant writing advertising copy for convenience product packaging. Tetra-pack boxes for wine, containers to drink yogurt in the car—what kind of world was I encouraging?

If I squinted at the blank, white hospital wall, I could be in my equally generic apartment. I remembered Tifi's North Carolina living room filled with books and souvenirs and musical instruments and plates of fresh macaroons and gingersnaps.

I had been topping my life with fat-free, faux-dairy

whip, and now I was being offered Devonshire cream.

Slowly, I folded the letter and returned it to the envelope through the frayed edge of my hasty opening. The plastic hospital bracelet caught on a spiky rip.

My name circled my wrist like a shackle. *Melissa.*

I tore it off.

CHAPTER 5

It was four blocks back to my apartment. I had the choice of taking a taxi or walking in my pajamas holding a pink envelope. I stood on the curb with the sliding glass doors of the hospital closing behind me, the nurse and wheelchair receding inside. Cool wind met my face in the fading light.

I decided to walk. Funny thing about a near-death experience, even if you only *thought* it was near-death: dying of embarrassment becomes a bit improbable.

Besides, I wasn't the only one on the street in pajamas. The Apocalypse Man shuffled back and forth at the next light. He was always shouting about the end of the world when I walked into the market for a box of sugar-free ice cream.

Today, even his greasy, matted hair was lifting in the wind, and he chopped his arms through the air at an imaginary adversary. When he saw me, he froze. He looked at me as though in recognition. Then he straightened to a salute. He pressed the crosswalk button for me, bowed, and walked away.

When the light changed, I continued toward home, thinking about France and only vaguely aware of the stares as I walked by, talking to myself.

"It's crazy. I can't get that time off work. And even if I could, I'd have to get my passport. Wait!"

A little lady looked up in surprise and moved to the edge of the sidewalk.

"I already have one!" In the bottom of my nightstand lay the unused passport from the last time Aunt Tifi had invited me. Something started to shift inside my spirit—something that didn't fit on the side of a plastic container.

The evening sky was clear as it darkened into the color of the sea I'd never seen. I was more familiar with the blue television light pulsing through my neighbors' curtains.

I started into my building as a man left it. I think he lived there, but I had never paid close attention. Like me, he practiced the art of ignoring and didn't glance at my attire as he held the door for me. I hoped Rolf had at least closed my door. The parts between sting and hospital were a blur. I ran up the stairs and saw the white of my closed door. I breathed a sigh of relief, visualizing a long, hot bath as I turned the knob.

Locked.

Our building wasn't fancy enough for a doorman, watchman, or anyone on site with an extra set of keys.

My extra key was tangled with paperclips in my desk drawer at the office. All of a sudden I was tired. Fantasies of French vacations and hot baths dissolved.

I turned and faced the empty hall and all the other white, closed doors. I didn't know my neighbors. The big woman with the Chihuahua lived two doors down. What would I say, "Can I sleep on your couch?"

I turned back down the stairs and out onto the sidewalk. The wind had ceased, but the starter trees still leaned in the direction of it, tied to their stakes. I walked across the parking lot to my little hatchback, expecting it to be locked, too.

To my surprise, it opened. I sat inside, tossed Tifi's letter onto the dashboard, and closed the door. We'd been having a mild spring. I could pretend I was camping. I crawled onto the backseat and reached into the hatch for the wool blanket I always kept for emergencies or picnics, neither of which had ever happened.

Back up in the driver's seat, I opened the glove compartment and found the granola-nut bar I'd left there yesterday. Here I was, having an emergency picnic in my parking lot. I laughed until I choked on an almond.

I let my seat fall as far back as it would go. Way beyond my rearview mirror, up above a well-lit penthouse, a dim star appeared.

Maybe where my French relatives lived, the stars were brighter than the electric lights.

❖

I woke to fogged windows and a numb leg. It was barely light enough to see Aunt Tifi's letter sitting on the dash, reflecting a pink version of itself into the windshield.

Slowly, I cranked my seat upright and looked at my face in the mirror. A deep indent ran down my left cheek. I looked away.

Good morning, me: hysterical hypochondriac who hospitalized herself, spent the night in her car, and was left stranded in her own parking lot.

I rubbed my neck, wondering at the constant in each of those circumstances. Fear. I was afraid of the bee, I was afraid of knocking on my neighbor's door.

I grabbed the letter and read it again as if looking for some clue.

Borage.

Storm.

Uncle Jean-Luc.

The proverbial light bulb came on. I opened my door and lurched out. I shook out a few kinks, ignored others, and then crouched down by the driver's door to feel along the bottom of the car body. When Uncle Jean-Luc had given me his old hatchback, he had shown me where he kept a magnetic key box. "Never drive anywhere without a spare key," he'd said. I had never needed it. Was it still there?

Yes and ick. By the feel of the grime, it had been there a long, long while. Wiping my hand on my sleeve,

I slid open the little container and dumped out the key into my palm. I laughed aloud. Then I remembered my car was dead. Still. . . . Sliding back into the driver's seat, I stuck the key in the ignition, whispered a prayer, and turned it.

It started. It started? And it sounded fine. I cranked up the heat and felt the hairs on my arms lift in the frigid blast of air. The goose bumps weren't just from the cold.

CHAPTER 6

Unlike my apartment complex, my office building did have a night watchman. By the time I arrived, it was just past six—a safe enough hour to get inside without being seen by anyone but Herman. Herman was smiling. Herman was always smiling.

"Hey there Miss Mel, I think you're a bit early for casual Friday."

"I'm a bit early, that's for sure. Herman I . . . forgot my keys. Do you mind letting me into the office?"

"Not at all. But then Elliot's already here."

Of all the days.

Herman's smile turned to one of schoolboy conspiracy. He whispered, "How 'bout I let you in the supply entrance 'round back."

I laughed. "Herman, you're an angel."

"Try convincing my wife."

Like two comic book characters, we tiptoed down the service hall and around to a gray door. With stage-like exaggeration and a wink, Herman let me in and left the door ajar. I found myself amid shelves stacked high with copier paper and ink toner. I opened the other door leading into the main office. For once, I was glad the cubicles were far away from the main offices I had spent six years working toward.

The room was dark except for Elliot's office light. I could easily get in and out without him seeing me.

I reached my cubicle and pulled open a drawer. Bingo. My spare key. I glanced at the top of my desk and saw a huge stack of papers. I felt a sticky note on top of them but couldn't read it in the dim light. Why bother? I gently closed the drawer and was turning to go when an overhead fluorescent light flickered on.

I stopped and saw Elliot standing with his hand on the light switch. He looked me up and down and then folded his arms.

"It must have been a good party. Did you bring your date?" He looked around with mock interest. "Good thing you came in early, albeit a bit underdressed. Paisley?" He laughed and shook his head. "Ever original, Mel. You've got a fair amount of work to catch up on. Since you missed the meeting, I took the liberty of volunteering you for the new Holman account. You're welcome."

I tightened my grip on the spare key. I could smell his expensive aftershave two cubicles away. The scent of it was a blend of tension, wariness, and disdain. I was tired of breathing it in.

Grabbing the edge of my desk, I leaned over the Holman account. The memo was now visible in the light: "One step closer to your own office?"

It was the question mark that did it. I started to look up at him, and my eye caught on a snapshot of my aunt and mother swinging me between them when I was in first grade. The picture was wedged between copyediting symbols and nutrition facts. I pulled it down and looked at it.

The aftershave intensified. "So, yesterday you were away because. . . ?"

I looked up and smiled. "Because I started my vacation."

And then, photo in one hand, key in the other, I walked away.

"Mom?"

"Hello, love."

"I'm going."

"Good. And Tifi's going to meet you in Marseille?"

"Essentially."

"Well, I'm glad you're finally getting on a plane. Your father would have been proud of you."

"For getting on a plane?"

"For taking a risk."

"Yeah, risky Mel. Doing what most people do without a thought. Hey, if you want to come to the city, you can stay at my place. And water the borage."

"The what?"

"Long story. Mom, am I crazy to go?"

"I hope you finally are . . . just a little bit."

CHAPTER 7

There was a reason I was afraid of flying. It wasn't natural for a big chunk of metal to lift up into the sky and cross an ocean. Knowing that the chunks of metal did so successfully most all of the time was no comfort—it was the inevitable unsuccessful times I worried about.

I was sitting in my window seat when the sleeping pills started to kick in. I kept checking my seat belt strap and craning my neck to make sure the nearest exit hadn't moved. *Breathe. Breathe.* In an odd combination of agitation and drowsiness, I clenched my jaw and yawned audibly. The woman next to me shook her newspaper.

Outside, men in large headphones were hauling baggage into the plane's belly. How was it possible to lift all of that and all of us into the air? When was the last trans-Atlantic crash?

Think of something else.

I had tried to get on a plane before, with Mr. Once. (That's what Aunt Tifi now called him. Not a bad idea, come to think of it.) She figured if she invited him along, I might fly. I had gotten as far as the carpeted boarding tunnel, felt it shift with the weight of the passengers, and had turned around and walked out.

Weakness hadn't gone over well with Mr. Once. We didn't exchange a single word on the drive back to the city. For Christmas that year, he'd bought me a model plane.

Another yawn. This wasn't so bad. Why hadn't I tried a sleeping pill before?

Outside the real plane, a pigeon landed on the wing and watched the suitcases. I had the brink of an epiphany, but like the pigeon, it dipped down and lifted off.

My eyes closed. In the sudden space between wakefulness and sleep, I saw pieces of the model plane gliding underwater. Each piece hovered separately, illumined in thick, golden light. The water was a river of honey.

I was trying to drink from the river when someone poked me in the elbow. I looked up at the flight attendant. My mouth was pasty and thick. "Could I get some water before takeoff?"

She stood back up. "Miss, the plane has landed. You must exit now."

"What? But I just. . . . In Paris?" I looked out the window and blinked. The baggage cart still stood outside, except now they were pulling bags off. I sat forward. I fixed my eyes on the terminal buildings. Different. The sky and light. Different. I looked back to the flight attendant. Same expression of frustration.

I gave her a brief smile. "Sleeping pills live up to their name." I tried to slide out of the seat.

"Ah, you don't like flying?"

"I don't know. This was my first flight, and I don't remember any of it."

She pulled my backpack down and helped me slide it up my arms. The extra weight sent me wobbling. She slung my purse over my shoulder and aimed me toward the exit.

I started down the aisle, slid on discarded magazines in first class, and finally made it up the carpeted tunnel. By the time I emerged into the Charles de Gaulle airport, I had regained most of my balance, and by the time I made it through customs—looking a bit worse than my passport photo—I felt almost human.

Travelers walked toward and past me, some in a hurry, others strolling. They were speaking different languages into cell phones, to each other, to children. I heard French, English, and the density of German.

I followed the multilingual signs to baggage claim and wheeled a cart to the snaking conveyor belt. Most people had left with their suitcases already. After scanning the pieces still gliding by, I found a spot near the flapping mouth that spit out bags.

Half an hour later, the belt jerked to a halt. A few unclaimed bags rocked to stillness like exhausted beetles on their backs. Plaid and ribbon'd beetles, none of them mine. Instead of being angry, I felt hollow and groggy.

I fished in my purse for my ticket stub with the baggage claim barcode stuck to it. A piece of paper fluttered to the floor, and I bent down to retrieve it. It was the address tag the agent had given me at the check-in counter—the tag I had forgotten to fill out and attach to my bag.

The hollow feeling turned to numbness. Not that I couldn't feel my digits and limbs, but I couldn't even feel the disappointment riding piggyback with me to the lost baggage office.

A pleasant but harried Max was not optimistic. According to his computer, my suitcase had made it to Paris.

"So it was stolen?" I imagined all of my good shoes, shirts, and skirts crammed into a Parisian thief's flea market stall.

"*C'est possible.* Or it is possible someone took the wrong bag."

"But I'm going straight to Marseille by train. I'm not staying in Paris." I was sure I sounded like a whining child.

He pulled out a claim form. "If we do not find it in three days, fill out this form and send to the address. Then maybe reimbursement."

I held the form out like a petition for something I wanted to hear.

Max gave me his business card. "If three days and still no bag, you call this number, OK?"

I finished the paperwork and asked which way to the trains. The numbness started its painful dissolve. The song "I love Paris" ran through my head, with one little change. As I followed the signs to the train, I kept hearing the lyrics: "I hate Paris in the springtime."

CHAPTER 8

Was it before or after the failed flight with Mr. Once? After—because of the pumpkin. That's right, autumn.

I had taken the 'L' to the Green City Market one Saturday. When I saw the array of pumpkins, I decided to get one for Mr. Once and leave it on his doorstep. I wanted him to smile when he returned from a day of golf with his difficult business partner. When I chose a fair-sized, fairy-tale pumpkin, I had forgotten I'd taken the train—and it was a distance from the nearest station to his house.

There isn't an elegant way to carry a pumpkin. Despite the chill of the air, I was fairly warm and thirsty by the time I arrived at his townhouse.

I decided to use the spare key and get a glass of water. Leaving the pumpkin on the doorstep, I let myself in. The hallway was dim and silent. Just in case, I called out, "Hello? Harvest delivery. Anyone here to sign for a pumpkin?" My voice echoed up the polished stairs.

I followed the hall to the kitchen and poured a tall glass of water. That was new: a faucet-mounted filter. The phone rang as I was washing my glass with purified water. By the time voicemail clicked on, I was back in the hallway across from Mr. Once's home office.

A woman's voice began to speak. I paused, hand on the knob of the front door.

"Hey there. I pulled strings and got us in for tonight." A little laugh. "I know, I know: I'm good. You can have my entire evening. Aren't you special? Now that *is* the question. . . ." A big laugh. "Ciao." The recording clicked off.

I hadn't moved. Slowly, I turned the door knob and stepped outside. I stood a moment on the stoop, looking at my feet. There sat the pumpkin, bright enough to be a smile. I picked it up, took it over to the neighbor's stoop, and headed back to the train.

My seat on the train from Paris faced backward. That might have something to do with the introspection. I laughed, and the little woman across from me looked up and smiled.

As the train left the station, the window filled with ties and tracks. The rail yard shot by as we picked up speed. Tracks joined and split, morphing into a time-release blossoming of the borage flowers.

This must be jet lag: being suspended in a tired awareness. I sighed and looked around me. The tube of the train body was compact and curved. A speeding bullet upholstered in green.

I glanced back at the woman across from me. She sat straight in her well-cut jacket, her neat, gray coif pinned to the top of her head. A paper bag lay on the window table between us.

Outside, industrial outskirts blurred past. I fished in my backpack for the books Aunt Tifi had packed at the base of the borage plant: a journal, a traveler's guide to French, and an English version of *The Little Prince*.

My aunt had read that story to me when I was in grade school. I remembered only the vague, mental backdrop I had created for a fictional boy who lived on a planet so small he could watch the sun set forty-four times a day.

Inside the book, Tifi had written:

Mel,

> *Do you remember this? You were seven the summer I read it to you. But no such fiction for Melissa. You told me you would hate living on a planet so small. Well, maybe you're ready for it now.*
>
> *It's one of my favorite books.*

Love, Aunt Tifi

P.S. I always wondered what the Prince ate? Did he

even have to? He seemed full with life, though. Let me
know what you think.

My stomach grumbled at the thought of food. I found a gummy energy bar in my purse, took one bite and tossed it in the little trash beneath the window table.

The woman across from me pointed at the paper bag and said something that I guessed referred to its contents. She reached inside the bag, pulled out two napkins, and then placed a cheese tart on top of each. She slid one in my direction.

I smiled. *"Merci.* Do you speak English?"

She shook her head, said something else and ended with *"Bon appétit."*

"Merci," I said again, losing the last vowel in a bite of flaky, creamy beauty. Whatever I'd been buying was certainly not cheese. My taste buds rejoiced. When finished, I licked my fingers and gave the woman a guilty shrug. She laughed and leaned back to sleep.

I opened *The Little Prince.* The story and the French landscape began to overlap. The Little Prince pulled out the baobab trees to keep his planet from turning to dust, and neighborhood gardens flew by. He visited asteroids occupied by eccentrics, and a business district approached and receded. He visited earth where other roses grew, and a hill rose to fill the train window with a wall of spring flowers.

For the first time on this journey, I was starting to feel good—or the possibility of goodness.

When I finished the book, one of its themes was dancing in my spirit: we can't see essential things with our eyes—only with our hearts.

I opened the blank journal, clicked open my pen and wrote: *Run a river of honey between us to sweeten every passage.*

A voice announced the next stop: Marseille.

PART THREE

Back along the Canal du Midi . . .

CHAPTER 9

"You sick of cars or something?" a voice asked above me.

I opened an eye to see Blaise leaning over me, his face upside down. Or was I upside down?

His mouth looked funny as it formed the words, "How you say," he snapped his fingers, "carsick?"

I shook my head, and everything twirled around again. Bad idea.

"No. It's not that." I lifted my head and scooted upright. Blaise came behind me, reached his hands under my armpits and heaved me to my feet. He kept a hand on the middle of my back as I tried my balance on the grass. I felt the fabric of my jacket stick to my shoulder blades.

I looked at the back of the truck to make sure this all wasn't a nightmare. The humming I'd heard before falling to the ground hadn't come from my head. It came from bees. A box of bees.

I shivered. "Bees. You keep *bees?*"

"You don't know this?" Blaise asked, keeping his hand out to steady me. "Tifi does not say this?"

"She never said much about Uncle Jean-Luc's work. Only that he had a small, family business in France." I wiped a chunk of mud off my elbow.

Blaise's worry assuaged, he rallied by telling me, *"Bien.* Then you stop being afraid."

For a second, I didn't realize he was referring to the bees. Rain rolled down my forehead and into my eyes. I turned to look at him. "Just like that? Stop? It doesn't work that way."

He shrugged and looked at his dead cigarette. "Why not? Beside, if you stay afraid, it's not good. The bees know when you are afraid of them." He tossed the cigarette into the gravel and slammed the truck's rear doors.

"It's not that easy." I straightened and turned to face him, fists to hips.

He came around the passenger door and opened it, reaching in with a grin. "No? Now you are angry and not afraid. Just—how you say—distract yourself. You want your things?" He held out my backpack in one hand and my purse in the other.

I stomped over to him and grabbed my purse, slinging it over my neck and shoulder. I felt the strap squish into my back. Blaise was smiling. He kept my backpack. "I carry this for you. Come." He crossed the gravel path to the barge's gangplank. I hesitated before following him.

"Be careful on the stairs," he called behind him. He reached the deck and then the wheelhouse. I noticed the barge faced back the way we had come. I guessed that meant east, toward the Mediterranean.

The stained-glass window above the wheelhouse door came into focus. Though the light coming from inside was dim, I could make out a cherub holding some kind of round container with leaded words scripted beneath.

Inside, the wheelhouse ceiling sloped in a graceful curve I could imagine sliding under an arched bridge. The polished wood of the steering wheel glowed in the lamp light. Blaise pulled off his jacket and hung it on a spoke before starting down the stairs. I followed him into the barge's belly, wondering how much of the cabin was under water. I bumped my head on the low lintel at the base of the stairs.

I was rubbing my forehead when Blaise stopped and pointed to a button on the wall which he pressed. "Here are lights. There is the galley." He gestured to his right at a kitchen in shades of brown and cream. He dumped my pack near the door and reached toward a little wine rack mounted to a wall above the chocolate-tiled counter. As he started to work a cork out, he punched on another light with his elbow. A sitting room came into view.

I entered the salon under a forty-watt bulb. Dark wooden paneling reached from white ceiling to blond wood floor. A braided oval rug filled most of the room. To the right of it stood a book shelf, flush with the walls and flanked by sagging, stuffed chairs. In the corner near the galley sat a green-tiled wood stove. A golden, upholstered booth ran under the windows on the left, providing seating for a polished table hinged to the wall. Clustered round the other side of the table were ladder-back chairs of varying finishes. A built-in divan of thread-bare velvet curved along the corner to my immediate left. Everything built in had the age and grace of the twenties. Everything else looked like the leftovers from a weekend yard sale in a low-rent neighborhood.

Blaise came up behind me, a glass in hand. The scent of nicotine clung to his shirt. "You like to sit?"

I accepted the glass. "No, thanks. I've been sitting for days." I skeptically sniffed my drink. It smelled gentle. "What is it?"

"Guess."

"Mead. So it's made with honey?"

"Mais oui." He held up his glass, "To the *mademoiselle* who will kill her fear. *Santé."*

"What does it mean, *santé?"*

"'To your health.' A toast." He looked me in the eyes as we clicked our glasses.

I brought the glass to my lips and then lowered it. "Where are Aunt Huguette and Uncle Gilbert? Don't they live on the barge?"

Blaise took a good swig of his drink. "Yes. *Les parents* live here, but tonight they are in the city, Carcassonne. No return until very late, I think. They apologize and tell me to show you the *péniche."*

He didn't seem in any hurry, though. Neither was I to taste his mead. I took a cautious sip of the drink and paused once it hit my tongue. *Hmm.* Tasted like fermented honey. Although I barely remembered the flavor of honey.

He smiled wide, "You like?"

"It's . . . er . . . good."

He laughed. "*Bien.* You know where the bottle is now."

I took another sip. It *was* good. "What will you do with the bees?"

Blaise shrugged. "Eh, I take care of it. You want to see your *cabine?*"

"Please. I'd like to shower." I patted the side of my head to feel for stray hairs and felt grit.

He retrieved my backpack and crossed the salon to a narrow hall running along the right side of the barge wall. I followed, observing where the light switches—buttons, rather—were in the wainscoting of veneered paneling. Tiny curtains, not much more than a foot long, covered round windows set high into the wall.

At the end of the hall, Blaise opened the last door on the left. It resisted and he pressed it in with his shoulder. He disappeared inside, and I hesitated at the doorway. He pressed the light on with his glass and surveyed the small space with its narrow bed along the facing wall. The head of the bed was hidden in an alcove made by the bathroom to the left. I saw more of Blaise than the cabin.

"So. All good for the night?" He asked, tossing my

pack on the bed. It dimpled the center of the puff comforter and partly disappeared. He took another drink of mead as I slung my purse off my shoulder and let it fall to the floor.

I held my glass in both hands. "Just dandy. Thanks."

He nodded and turned for the door. I backed out to let him through, and he clicked his glass against my knuckles as he passed, turning toward the curtain hanging at the end of the hall.

I was going to be alone on a barge. I turned and started to follow him. "Do you live nearby?"

"Almost next door. The old lock house across the canal. There is a little bridge across. I can hear if you yell." Holding the curtain back, he looked at me for a second. "You are not so afraid, Melissa?" He lifted his glass to encompass the barge, the night, two relative strangers on a dark barge.

I smiled and shook my head. "No, I think I'll try to distract myself. Like you suggested."

"Let me know if you need other distractions." And with a wink, he disappeared through a door and onto a staircase I glimpsed for a second before the curtain fell back into place, swaying as if we were at sea.

CHAPTER 10

After Blaise's footsteps left the deck for shore, I turned to survey my cabin again. The bathroom was smaller than my closet at home, the sink about the size of a salad bowl. The floors and walls and even the ceiling were tiled in a pale blue. I stepped inside to peek at the shower and knocked my hip on the towel rack and my shin on the wastebasket.

I turned and followed the path Blaise had sent my backpack, flopping onto the bed. On impact, I stiffened. The comforter might live up to its name, but not the bed springs.

I rose to kneeling and opened the little, round window above the bed. In rushed the damp and cold night. I closed my eyes and felt the air, delicious on my tired, dirty skin. I took in the view from my porthole and found myself on eye level with the canal's edge, facing the hood of the parked Renault.

I heard Blaise move cross the gangplank to shore,

talking fast but soft. I heard a few impatient *"oui's"* and the sound of a cell phone flipping closed. He came into view on the bank, a dark silhouette raising an arm toward the canal and gesturing impatiently for someone to come toward him.

Another man appeared, hands in his pockets. They faced each other in silence a moment before Blaise nodded toward the truck and said something. The other man shrugged, tugged on his ear and followed Blaise around to the back of the Renault. The back doors opened and the truck heaved.

Both men reappeared alongside the truck, carrying a large box between them. They headed for the barge. I ducked back and swallowed, letting the window close a bit.

They were bringing the bees *on board*.

Distraction.

How about learning French? I pulled the pocket-sized French book out of my backpack as I heard the shuffle of feet on deck.

"Je m'appelle Melissa."

A muffled thud sounded over my head followed by retreating footsteps.

"Comment vous appellez-vous?"

I was left alone on a barge. With a box of bees.

Quelle horreur!

CHAPTER 11

I woke to the sound of angel wings beating. The darkness of night broke the dream. I fumbled for my bed-side light, and banged my hand into a wall. A wall? I shook my hand out and sat halfway up. What was normally a night stand had turned into paneling.

Barge, not apartment.

Just as I found the lamp chain, I heard the sound again. Not wings, feet. I left myself in the dark. Thieves? My body stung with goose bumps, my mind lurched at memory.

A man's voice, lowered, came from the hall. A woman's voice answered, not so softly. Someone paused in front of my door and then retreated back down the hall.

My aunt and uncle had returned.

After lying still a few minutes longer, I pressed on the light and crawled out of bed, attempting chronology. Had I fallen asleep studying French? No, the light was off. Aha. I remembered. I had battled the calcified shower head and crispy towels and had sent Aunt Tifi a prayer of thanks for telling me to pack pajamas in my carry-on.

I found my watch and synched it to the clock on the wall. One a.m. I was wide awake.

I didn't feel like learning any more French phrases. Instead, I picked up my journal. The line I'd jotted in the train surprised me. I had barely written anything but marketing reports and product labels since the year after I'd graduated from college.

That year, several writers and I had spent many happy hours between part-time jobs at a tiny Laotian restaurant, nursing tea and trying to create a poetry review. But not long after the camera flashes at graduation had dimmed, our eyes dilated with student loans and everyone's idea of adulthood.

That's when I'd met Mr. Once. He had walked into the Laotian restaurant to order beef soup and spring rolls. I sat at the window table, the red neon of the "open" sign giving my papers an odd glow. I saw him before he entered. He noticed me after he ordered, when he came back to the condiment stand and shook sesame seeds onto his soup.

He looked over at my papers. "Looks like you took work home with you."

"Something like that."

He pulled a pair of disposable chopsticks out of their paper wrapper and broke them apart evenly, perfectly, without looking. Mine were uneven, as always, like a wishbone. He pointed at me with the sticks. "Good girl, that's the way to get a raise."

I laughed. "Not at a poetry review."

He pulled one napkin out of the dispenser. "Do you write?" Another napkin.

"Yes."

"I know of a place looking to hire a writer. Technical stuff, but decent money. Room for growth."

I fished for the last noodle in my cup of soup. Ordering the cup was less expensive than the bowl. Even at a hole-in-the wall eatery, I ordered the cheapest thing on the menu. My school loan payments were going to kick in soon. My rent was past due. All the prosaic and unpoetic necessities.

Years and miles later, on a strange barge in France, I tried to remember what it had been like to love my work. When I thought nothing of shopping at thrift stores and going to gallery openings for free *hors d'oeuvres*. When reward was a not a direct-deposit, year-end bonus, but that silvery feeling of surprise at a string of words more satisfying than pearls. I picked up my pen. Instead of inspiration, frustration. The poetry seemed to have expired on the train. I wrote:

> *I buy shoes designed for dancing and have only walked in them. I go to the gym to cancel out cheese, spinning away my energy on a bike bolted to a floor. I use night cream made from moon dust to keep away wrinkles from the sun I never see.*
>
> *I am tired of something.*

Perhaps it is myself.

❖

I awoke with my journal clasped to my chest. Natural light and plenty of dust motes filtered into my cabin. I yawned and stretched my arms up, sending the motes dancing toward the ceiling and my journal cartwheeling to the floor. I sat up and sniffed then coughed.

Not motes, *smoke.*

I plummeted out of bed and tripped on my covers, landing on the floor. My hands reached the door, and I felt it. Cold. I slid my nose to the crack beneath it. Nothing there. I retrieved my ankles from twisted sheets and pressed the door lever down, looking back at the strand of smoke wafting in from the window.

In the hall to my left was the curtained door Blaise had used last night. Had he dropped a cigarette somewhere? I yanked aside the curtain and almost ran into the door. I pushed the lever down, expecting to shove it open like every other door I had encountered thus far. It flung easily open, sending me flying up the stairs and onto the deck into a swirl of smoke.

Smoke and bees.

CHAPTER 12

I stood paralyzed in paisley. Even the sky was paisley—swirling plumes of smoke spiraled up and over stacked wooden boxes. I started coughing and heard a man yelling in French over a loud noise. I closed my eyes against the stinging smoke and covered my mouth with one hand, waving at the smoke with the other.

A woman's voice joined the man's, closer by. A hand landed on my arm and tugged me. I squinted an eye open and still saw only smoke. Looking down, in the direction of the hand, I saw a short, square woman in white gesturing toward mid-ship. I stumbled after her, coughing.

She stopped, and I opened my eyes completely. The smoke shifted, no longer blowing straight at me. We were on the other side of the stacked boxes and netting. The woman turned to reach down into a bucket, yelling to the man, also in white. He was poking at long cylinders of rolled cardboard that smoked profusely from both ends through bits of pine needles sticking out.

I wasn't going to burn to death after all. But a vague discomfort still clung to me. It must be the noise. A sound like television static at full volume. The woman, my Aunt Huguette, handed me a damp cloth, and a glass of water. I took a deep drink and wiped my face. Over the din I started to say, "Thank you, I. . . . " And then I registered the bees.

Instead of sky, a swarm of bees filled the space between the barge and the tops of the trees lining the canal. I looked up and up, my lower jaw remaining down as my head fell back, mouth open, in amazement and horror. The edge of a memory came forward, but I slammed it back, unable to deal with more than this moment.

My aunt and uncle, whom I'd still not officially met, continued to prime the smoking sticks. As the smoke increased, the bee swarm decreased. I remained immobile as the bees began to quiet themselves and fly inside the wooden boxes.

The dozens and dozens of boxes on deck were hives.

❖

"Are you hungry, Melissa?" Gilbert asked, kissing my cheeks in greeting. Did I look hungry? If I looked like I felt, he would be asking if I was human.

Huguette frowned, pushing him away. "You make

64

her filthy, idiot." She said as she brushed us both off simultaneously. Gilbert was smudged with soot. He pulled off his white jacket.

Gilbert gave me a wink and checked to see if his wife had noticed. She stood back with a deeper frown, hands on hips. *"Mais* you never change!" She heaved a hand up near his nose. "You go wash. Now."

"Oc, oc." He said.

Oc?

Huguette turned me to face her by reaching for my shoulders. She looked me up and down and then clasped her hands, pronouncing, *"Oc,* you look like Tifi. It is there. The big nose."

She turned toward the wheelhouse. Over her shoulder she said, "Come, we have breakfast."

Tifi. Aunt Tifi had *known* they kept bees. Ooo, if she were here, I'd. . . .

"Come, come." Huguette was waiting for me at the door to the wheelhouse, gesturing for me to follow her. I finally moved.

The stained glass over the wheelhouse door was radiant with daylight. I paused to look closer at the image. The cherub held a rounded beehive with one arm. He sucked honey from his finger. Beneath the pudgy angel, steep and wide art deco letters read: *"Sprüche* 24:13-14."

"Melissa!" I heard Huguette's voice on the same stairs Blaise had led me down the night before.

I entered and carefully ducked this time as I descended. I heard singing and smelled coffee before I reached the bottom. I peeked into the galley to see Gilbert slathering butter on opened baguette. Huguette handed me a wooden tray with a press pot of coffee and a stack of cream-colored, ceramic bowls. She jerked her head in the direction of the salon. "Too cold for breakfast on deck this morning. Too much smoke too." She directed this last statement at Gilbert who started singing louder.

My legs still coursed with adrenaline. I took the tray into the salon, trying not to drop it. I set it down and went to warm my hands by the old, green-tiled stove. It was cozy here. If I didn't think about the bees.

Huguette entered with a tray of the buttered bread and jars of honey. She gestured for me to sit and placed a piece of baguette in front of me. *"Tranchoir.* You know?" She scooted in at the end of the red booth and poured coffee into the bowls.

Gilbert joined us at the head of the table and promptly folded his hands. Huguette followed suit, and so did I. His words of grace sounded like a conversation between friends.

Huguette joined Gilbert's "Amen" and then continued as if the prayer hadn't happened. *"Tranchoir.* You speak *any* French? We all learned English. We sell honey to the tourists—the Dutch, the Germans, many Europeans. *They* all learn English too."

I wasn't interested in language at the moment. "Why were you smoking the bees?"

"It is to calm them," Gilbert said, as he drizzled one of the honeys across his bread. He then cut it into pieces and floated them in his coffee. "Bees get upset sometimes." He dunked the little bread boats in his bowl and pointed to them with his spoon: "*Petits bâteaux.* Little boats." He laughed without much sound, the lines of his mouth stretching wide and linking to other sun-deep lines around his face.

Huguette mumbled something and rolled her eyes. "Here, try the honey. This one is lavender."

I held the little jar. Last night, I'd tasted mead and slept beneath bees. This morning, I'd walked through swarming hives unscathed. I supposed I could combine a building sense of "why not?" with atonement for my lack of French and give the honey a try. I lifted a running strand of honey from the wooden stick, spun it back and forth, and drizzled it over my bread. The sweetness fell onto the butter, sliding off to catch on the exposed, soft insides of the bread. I took a bite of my *tranchoir* and was amazed that three flavors could taste so divine.

I had been keeping this sweetness out of my life, deliberately. I felt a brief surge of compassion for the little girl who had decided to hate bees and their honey.

Huguette had been watching me. She nodded. "The bees are disturbed sometimes when a new queen bee is coming to the hive. And we were not here last night to welcome her. All this strangeness, our *abeilles* were not happy."

I swallowed carefully. "The *abeilles*—they live on the boat? All the time?"

"But of course." Huguette set down her bowl of

coffee. "We keep bees, how else. . . ." She squinted. "You do not know we keep bees?"

Gilbert had finally found something worth looking up for. "But Tifi say you were coming to learn to make honey. That you wanted to. . . . " he looked at Huguette, "what did she say?"

It was my turn to avoid eye contact. I stared at Gilbert's bowl where the last piece of bread was submerging.

"To 'taste and see.'" Huguette said it as if it were the most normal reason for an adventure.

"'Taste and see,'" Gilbert repeated as his last *bateau* sank completely into his coffee.

CHAPTER 13

I cleared my throat. "Aunt Tifi didn't say anything about you two keeping bees. Come to think of it, she never said exactly what kind of work Uncle Jean-Luc did. Something about sales for a family business."

At this, Huguette leaned back and crossed her arms. *"Incredible.* Gilbert's brother designed the labels for our honey. He sold in all the markets along the Canal du Midi. He was known from here to the Sea. *Just* sales for business? *Pfft."*

"She always talked about Uncle Jean-Luc with the greatest affection. You know how much she loved him. She used to tell the most wonderful stories about traveling with him in France." I decided to skip the fact that Aunt Tifi had omitted the entire barge and apiary from her stories. Hadn't she stayed here? I looked at Huguette ripping the last of her bread and wondered.

I turned to Gilbert, "And when is Tifi coming? Maybe she can explain herself."

"Tifi coming? Where, here?" Gilbert looked at me with a smile.

Aunt Tifi was bad with dates, but really. "She's not coming?"

Huguette filled her sturdy lungs with air and lifted a thumb. "First, Tifi *never* say when she comes. That enough is bad. Second," she lifted her index finger, "she never stay on the *péniche.*" She pursed her lips and lifted her chin. "What, we are not good enough for the American?"

Gilbert cleared his throat and smiled at me. I smiled back and tried not to laugh into my bowl. Huguette continued, "Always, she stays in a *pension.* . . ."

Gilbert cleared his throat more loudly. "Huguette, sometimes people have reasons we do not understand. Let us enjoy our niece, eh? If Tifi comes, she comes. You always keep the rooms perfect clean. So no problem if last minute." He looked at me. "It is lovely here on the *Honigschlecker,* yes?"

"This barge is absolutely lovely. No question about it. The *Honig*-what? It sounds like German."

Huguette started to gather the breakfast things and stack them on the tray. She looked up, "So you know the German word for honey. But you don't know the French?"

If Aunt Tifi hadn't stayed on the barge, I didn't blame her.

Gilbert answered both of us. "*Honigschlecker* means in English 'honeylicker.' It is a hard word for the French to say. It has a story. . . ."

70

Huguette cut him off, "Honey in French is *miel.*"

"*Miel,* I repeated.

Standing up, she pointed a crust of breakfast at me across the loaded tray. "Your name even means bees, you know this?"

I stood up and took the tray from her. "Yes. That I have learned."

After I helped her clean the breakfast dishes, Huguette followed me down the hall to my room. I entered and cringed, forgetting how I'd left it. She shook her head at the mess of my bedding and then lifted her foot. She had stepped in the puddle of clothes I'd left on the floor last night.

I felt like a child who'd failed room inspection. "I'm sorry, I'll clean it up." I reached for the bed and started smoothing things over. "I thought there was a fire on board when I woke up."

Huguette was already picking up my clothes and bundling them under her arm. She pointed to the wadding they had become. "I wash." She turned to go.

I turned from my bed, "Wait, those are the only clothes I have. My bag was lost. I just have those and these." I pointed to my pajamas.

Huguette sniffed the bundle under her arm and shook her head. "I wash," she repeated. "I borrow you some clothes." And with that, she turned on her heel.

Five minutes, later she returned with an armload of

polyester and faux denim. She deposited this unpromising combination on the bed, patted it, and said, "Come up when you are dressed."

I sighed, lifted a shirt from the pile, and held it up to myself. It was twice as wide as I and covered in green stripes—horizontal, kelly-green stripes.

And I'd thought all French women had fashion savvy.

CHAPTER 14

"Savvy, baby. It's all about the savvy. Turn." Mr. Once spun me around outside the dressing room, the Neiman-Marcus saleswoman standing by. He turned to her. "Do you think she can wear this color, or does it wash her out?"

"She," I said, hands on hips, "thinks it's absolutely awful."

The saleswoman studied me. "Perhaps the chartreuse."

"I draw the line at chartreuse. Sorry." I turned to Mr. Once. "I liked the first one."

He looked at me for a second. "It's rather boring, don't you think?"

The saleswoman pointed at her display case. "We have some strident accessories if you want to wake it up."

I stared at the woman. "Strident's not exactly the look I'm aiming for."

Mr. Once winked at her. "She hasn't gotten in touch with her inner ninja."

I had a choice: go with humor and do my best imitation of the Karate Kid's stance or refuse to pretend I found this exchange humorous and go change.

With his infuriating ability to read my mind, Mr. Once stroked his chin and asked. "What say you, Mel: Karate Kid or cardigan?"

Far away in France, I kicked a Perma-pleated pant leg high in the direction of the tiny bathroom mirror. "Mr. Miyagi wore cardigans, didn't he?"

I craned to see my torso. "But probably not the green stripes underneath."

I left my room and paused outside the door. Still peeved at Mr. Once and the long-ago ninja comment, I decided to use the prow stairs leading to the hives.

I emerged above deck directly onto an irregular pathway formed of stacked hives. I barely remembered anything about the morning's ascent except the swarming bees. In comparison, they now seemed well mannered. They arced and danced above the hive entrances, minding their business.

It was one thing to decide to walk through a city of bees. It was another to actually do it. As I walked slowly, I tried not to brush off the bees landing on my arms. *Keep moving,* I told myself.

The path curved around and opened onto a jumble of equipment and the wheelhouse beyond. When I emerged from the hive boxes, I relaxed enough to notice they were of all colors and sizes. Green netting, tacked to poles around the barge's edges, extended about four feet above the highest sections.

I could see Gilbert bending over his smoker. A man was sneaking up behind him with a smile. He had the same dark coloring as Blaise, but his frame was more solid.

I was about to call out when the man saw me and held his finger to his lips. Poised behind Gilbert, the stranger gripped the older man's shoulders. Gilbert jumped, grasping his chest. He turned and laughed when he saw who it was. They exchanged greetings in French, and then the other man looked toward me again and called out, *"Bonjour."*

I glanced down at the green stripes and Perma-pleats I was wearing. I actually hesitated—almost more willing to remain amid the bees than to be fully seen in the horrific, borrowed outfit. Maybe distraction did help.

Gilbert hailed me, "Melissa, this is my oldest son, Chance. You remember, yes?"

I stepped closer in curiosity. Chance? *This* was Chance? Last time I'd seen him, he had been a slouching, rangy teenager. This man stood in casual elegance and confidence.

Gilbert patted his son's shoulder and then mine. "And you remember Melissa. Tifi's niece. You met in

America."

Chance was watching me. He smiled and said, "So the queen has arrived." His English held only the faintest trace of an accent. It had improved. He leaned over to greet me with two kisses.

I just stood there. "Queen? Oh, you mean the queen bee. No, I was only the unknowing escort. *Bonjour.*" I was nervous. Why on earth did I feel nervous?

I caught him looking at the green-and-white stripes. I crossed my arms. "How many years ago did you stay with Tifi?"

"Over a dozen, I should think. You've grown up."

I wondered if he had. "Still partial to chili powder?"

He looked puzzled.

"Bonjour, cheri!" Huguette appeared through the wheelhouse door and greeted her son. He bent over to hug her, his shoulder blades rubbing against his thin, black sweater. Huguette broke the embrace and stepped back, still talking and now pointing to the bee colonies. Chance and his father exchanged a glance of resigned exasperation.

Gilbert turned to me, "Melissa, you want to help feed the bees?"

I tried hard to keep my face from blanching. I might be able to walk around them without breaking into hives—I almost laughed at my own pun—but feeding them? No.

Huguette reached for a bucket.

Chance was watching me. "Blaise mentioned you lost your bag. I have to make a delivery in Carcassonne if you want to get some things."

He took the bucket from his mother. "Though your clothing is quite striking on her, *Maman.*"

Huguette took the bucket back. "Go tomorrow. Then you can pick up new netting from Jacques." She pointed to a drooping strip of green sagging from a ripped section. She continued with a barrage of French, using the bucket for punctuation.

Chance caught the bucket mid-swing and set it down with a laugh. "Let's all take a walk. That way, you can see what's blooming, and we can show Melissa the village."

His parents seemed to think this a fine idea, and they started off the barge. Chance turned to me. In a low voice he asked, "You are afraid of the bees?"

"Shouldn't I be wearing protective clothing? Gloves? What if they sting?"

He smiled and reached toward the mouth of a hive. "Don't think of what you hate. Think of what you love."

A bee stepped off the wood and flickered across the tip of his finger. He held it toward me. It seemed both brothers had easy remedies for my life. They unsettled me. I looked Chance in the eyes without speaking, clasped my hands behind my back, and followed his parents to the shore.

CHAPTER 15

Standing on the canal bank, I had a more open view of the barge's mooring. On the shore to my right, a haphazard field of wildflowers overtook a garden and then disappeared into trees where the canal curved out of sight.

Up and to the left wound the drive we had descended last night. It led past a picturesque jumble of buildings. The tallest one rose several stories from high grass and a scattering of rusty equipment and machinery. Though the building was industrial, its workmanship was beautiful. Each window and door lintel was curved and carved with *bas relief* designs.

Between the taller structure and the canal sat a rambling, stone restaurant with a windmill gently dipping into the water. The canal continued uphill via a terraced lock. Huguette and Gilbert were crossing a footbridge that spanned it.

Chance passed me and pointed, "You are familiar

with locks? Come."

He started up the path, and I followed, curious. Cadmium red poppies, their petals splayed wide, opened their black eyes to the sun. The clouds had slipped, invisible, beyond the tops of trees.

Once on the footbridge, I could see down into a large, oval-shaped cavity, wide enough for a single barge. The water level was low, and the exposed stone walls were covered in dark moss.

Chance rested his elbows on the railing. "The locks function by motors that open doors under water. In the past, all were hand-cranked. Now, most are electronic." He pointed down. "The lock doors are V-shaped—better for water pressure. The lock itself is in the shape of an *amande.*"

"Almond."

He nodded. "It is for use and beauty. Use for the earth's pressure." He looked across the canal to the path his parents were walking on.

"And beauty for what?" I crossed the bridge to a large, gravel path wide enough for a single car. I didn't wait for an answer, but nodded at the other shore to a plaster-colored house with green shutters. "Is that the lock house?"

Chance looked as if he was deciding which of my questions to answer. He stuffed his hands in his pockets. "Each lock house on the canal has the same green shutters and a plaque. The plaque tells the canal distance in kilometers from Toulouse, so you always know how far you are from the Sea."

The door below the polished plaque was flanked by hanging pots of flowers. Green ivy framed the edges of the white building. It was the house I had imagined his parents would live in. "Your brother mentioned he lived there."

"*Oui*. And I as well. My family grew up in this house. The barge first belonged to my grandparents. They traveled up and down the canal, following the seasonal flowers and selling honey at the markets along the way. When they died, my father wanted to keep the bees." He shook his head, smiling. "That was an argument. My mother's family has run the lock house since it was built. To compromise, my brother and I promised to continue."

"And now you are lockkeepers."

"Something like that. We both have other things we want to do, so a village boy helps."

"Blaise mentioned he wants to make mead. And you want to cook." It wasn't exactly a question, and Chance didn't answer it, continuing to walk instead. It seemed we both had subjects we'd rather avoid.

Well then, I'd make it easy. "I like knowing the history of a place."

He kicked a large stone from the path into the water. "This was once a tow path. Horses pulled the barges up and down the canal. The builder of the canal realized: six horses could pull 3,000 kilos of goods over land. But six horses pulling a barge on water? Then they could pull 300,000 kilos."

I looked at the soft banks holding the water gently

between them. "So much back-breaking work to create ease for the future."

"It was built to connect the river in Toulouse with the Mediterranean Sea. Then it was for trade. Now it is for leisure travel."

"And for floating apiaries."

"One apiary. Ours is the last. This way." We had come to a stucco building with *Coopérative* painted in block letters across its front. Chance started down an abbreviated staircase.

When we emerged from beneath the trees, Chance stopped. "Look."

The sun split a low bank of steely blue clouds whose heavy bellies hung over a distant line of pines. Between us and the trees, a field opened wide, brimming with spring daisies and poppies and purple flowers I couldn't name. I bent over to touch a yellow petal. Chance walked around and past me into the flowers. He turned, arms wide, "This is the *douce France*. The 'gentle France.'"

Standing on the edge of the flowers, I looked out at the acres and acres of them turning their faces to the sun. Perhaps beauty needed no reason.

Chance turned and waved toward the middle of the field. I looked beyond his arm and saw his parents waving back.

"What are they doing?" I asked, wading into the flowers. Their damp petals brushed against my bare calves, morning dew melting on my skin.

"They are doing what they do best—arguing about

things they cannot control. Right now, I am guessing they debate whether the bees will produce enough honey. Huguette is loud, and Gilbert is quiet. . . ." The smile that lifted into his cheeks settled into a neutral line. "They are getting old." He pulled on his ear.

"You were the one who came last night to help Blaise with the queen bee."

"I was."

"And he told you I was afraid of them."

He nodded and bent over to pick a poppy. He reached toward my face with it, but I ducked to the side, laughing. "You must think I'm pathetic."

"On the contrary, I think you are brave." Chance was still holding the flower. I stood still. He reached again toward my face and slipped the poppy between my ear and temple. He started walking through the sunlight toward his parents.

I felt for the bloom, alien and fragile. I could almost hear it.

CHAPTER 16

Winter. The edge of a gray and frozen parking lot. I stomped my feet to keep them warm, looking up to where the sun should be.

Mr. Once was already looking away, his blond hair lifting stiffly in the wind. He never wore hats. He sniffed. "Don't blame me."

"I don't." I did. But if I said anything, he would turn cold as the cement beneath my boots. No wool socks could delay such chill.

He looked at me, finally, pursing the lips of that mouth that could kiss and cut in the same breath.

If I put my arms over his shoulders and smiled. If I kissed him. These were the "if's" I knew the "then's" for. But if I stood here, letting him choose?

He reached a glove to my ear and patted it. I heard the brown leather glance off my lobe where it stuck out from beneath my hat.

The glove returned to his pocket, "Fine then. See

you at the party?"

"I'll be visiting my mom, remember?"

"Right, right. Have fun. Need a ride back?"

My eyelashes were damp with frost. I wanted to wipe them off, but I didn't want him to think I was crying. "No. I'd like to walk. Thanks."

A shrug. He was already walking toward his car, holding out his remote key. The Audi beeped and its headlights flashed.

I held up a hand. I wasn't sure if I was dismissing him or saying goodbye.

"You are looking pretty with a flower in your hair," Gilbert told me when I reached the couple. Chance was a few strides ahead of me being harangued by his mother.

To Gilbert, I said, *"Merci.* Is there anything I can help with today?" He squeezed my shoulder and looked at his wife and son. Huguette waved her short and thick arms in all directions as Chance crossed his. The son had inherited his mother's ramrod-straight posture. Chance towered over her, but it was difficult to say who looked more imposing.

Gilbert sighed. "I am sure Huguette will think of something."

At her name, Huguette waved off her son's last comment and faced us. "Yes. We check the hives for mites."

Gilbert inched his shoulders up and turned back toward the barge. Chance was trying not to laugh. Huguette stomped after her husband, calling something to her son over her shoulder. I was still wondering why we had all walked out into the field.

Chance translated, "We are requested to go to the market and get some things for lunch."

The sun warmed my throat and hands. I wanted to stay right where I was. Chance started back toward the tall line of plane trees.

I came up beside him and pointed at the line of green. "Your canal is like a secret. Unless you know she is there, you don't know how to look for her."

"Ah, the American is a poet."

"If she ever wrote any poetry, perhaps. How often do your parents move the barge?"

"When they took over the *Honigschlecker*, they did not want to lose our community—our church, our school. So they bought the old mill with Gilbert's inheritance and kept the boat here. Our family has been arguing about what to do with the mill ever since. There had been a restaurant in the smaller building before the Second World War. Years ago, they rented it to Emil. Keeping bees is not exactly, how do you say . . . lucrative?"

He pointed toward the church spire on a hill behind the canal. "That is north," he said. "The canal runs mostly east-west, and we are on the eastern outskirt of the village. Outskirt. I liked learning that word. I imagine a woman twirling her skirt. The barge is moored at the seam of her hem."

"Ah, the Frenchman is a poet."

He laughed. "No, not even if I wrote. My brother, though? Maybe him."

We ascended the bank farther up the tow path than where we had left it earlier. Here, the canal formed a small harbor. Barges and boats rested on the green surface of the water. A man in wrinkles and a sea cap walked by holding a bare baguette by a slip of wax paper.

The harbor's western side pinched off under a narrow bridge. Beyond it, the canal curved north around the edge of the village. At its eastern side, the harbor narrowed in the direction of the *Honigschlecker*. Just visible through the arc of trees were the mill restaurant and the lock.

Chance was watching me with the smile of a tour guide whose tourist appreciates the terrain. And who wouldn't appreciate it? This was the periphery of a fairy tale, this provincial village.

"Is this part of Provence?" I asked.

"You haven't been reading your guidebook. It's called the Languedoc. The name comes from *langue d'oc,* literally: 'the language of *Oc,*' or *Occitan*. In the north was the *langue d'oïl*. Both *oc* and *oïl* mean 'yes.'"

"The second one sounds like *oui*."

"And it is—or turned into it. Many of the younger people here say *oui*. *Oc* is not as common anymore."

"So you speak the language of 'yes.' I like that."

"As do I. We are proud of our language and

heritage. And here in the Languedoc, part of that heritage is our *cassoulet* and the troubadours, among other things."

"You *are* a walking encyclopedia, aren't you?"

"My apologies. I get carried away."

"It's a compliment. Keep going. Though I know what *cassoulet* and troubadours are."

"I would argue that you do not yet know true *cassoulet*, something we will soon fix. And troubadours? Yes, I think you know these. I think you are one."

I laughed. "Not if you heard me sing."

"Oh, the spirit of the troubadour is poetry. Poetry is the song of the spirit. Here we are."

We had passed the southern end of the bridge and stood in front of a small *Fruits et Légumes* shop. I was captivated by the pyramids of lemons and the architectural stacks of cucumbers.

Chance held up a cluster of grapes. "You like? Try one."

I pulled off one of the dusty-looking grapes, and it turned shiny between my fingers. "I've never seen grapes like this. In the supermarkets, they look polished." I popped it in my mouth, enjoying the tight, clear burst of flavor.

"French supermarkets, too. But all of this comes from our neighbors' farms. It is how villages have grown and sold for ages. Actually, your America is full of organic growers and co-op's." He set an ornate head of lettuce next to the grapes on the counter.

"And you noticed this on your high school visit?"

He laughed. "No, in Southern Oregon. I worked on an organic farm there after university. Some of us French do like your country."

I looked up from the bananas stacked with their curves convex. "I haven't even been to Oregon. Or to the West Coast, for that matter."

"It is lovely. Like northern California without as many people. Yet."

"What took you there, specifically?"

He paid the stout woman behind the counter who was talking with a friend. She greeted Chance and smiled at my green-and-white shirt. Hers was the same but in red. As we left, Chance answered me. "My great-grandfather, Pascal-Desire, started a vineyard there."

"You're kidding. In Oregon?"

"Near a little village called Jacksonville. About as large as this town. He had a small farm—on the hem of the skirt of Jacksonville."

I spun around on the spot. "I'm twirling the hem of my imaginary skirt. In reality, your mother's wide-leg pants."

He laughed, and this time I saw that two of his upper teeth were crooked. Back home, my co-workers had straightened and whitened their smiles to matching perfection. Chance's smile was perfect in a different way.

In the next-door shop window, a faded pink ceramic pig was doing a permanent jig. In the display cases, neat rows of sliced meats and symmetric lumps looked a lot different than the packaged ham I usually bought. The butcher greeted us with a warm welcome and then retreated into the back, emerging with a bundle wrapped in brown paper which he handed to Chance.

I reached for the bag from the vegetable shop. "Here, let me carry that one. I never knew you had returned to America."

Chance looked straight ahead. "I didn't tell you. Didn't think I'd made the greatest first impression."

"No. You didn't."

He looked at me with a definite twinkle in his eye. "Good thing we all grow up."

We were back alongside the canal. "Pascal-Desire, you really name people 'desire'?"

"Me personally?" Chance laughed and then tilted his head. "Why not. Most people don't know what they desire. If you give it a name, perhaps you call it into being."

Without thinking, I asked, "What do you desire?"

Chance gave me a smile large enough to crinkle his nose. "If you want me to answer that, you must also."

"Then your desires are safe secrets because I have no idea what mine are."

CHAPTER 17

Huguette waved to Chance from the deck of the barge. She met us on the bank and came over to inspect the purchases. She circled a finger in the air above the groceries to indicate them all, asking a final question. She narrowed her eyes and waited for the response.

Chance answered what sounded like a number. His mother kept her eyes slit, moving her lips in addition. She nodded finally, approving the total cost. She turned on her heel and headed back up the plank. Chance turned to me and winked.

He said in a low voice, trying not to laugh, "I learned when I was eight to say that things had been on sale, otherwise I'd be accused of squandering the grocery money."

We climbed on board the *Honigschlecker*. Huguette descended through the wheelhouse as Gilbert emerged from the bee boxes. He waved and turned back to the hives. Chance watched his father crouching over one of the boxes.

I held out my arm for the butcher's package. "Here, let me take everything down. I'll help her put things away."

He smiled, released the bags, and went to lift the box Gilbert was reaching for.

Huguette was down in the galley. She turned around and simply said, *"Bien,"* taking the bags from me. I joined her at the counter and helped her pull out fruit, lettuce, eggs.

Holding the carton of eggs, I asked, "Where is the fridge?"

She looked at me, the plane of her face tilted up toward mine. "What is this?"

"Fridge. Refrigerator." I lifted the eggs a bit.

"Mais non. Leave there."

Huguette pulled out the butcher's package and reached up to open a cupboard. At least it looked like a cupboard. The wooden door disguised a fridge the size of the one I'd had in my college dorm. I peeked over her shoulder in time to see the inside packed with little jars and knotted bags before Huguette shoved the door shut and turned to find me there.

I backed away and picked up the head of lettuce, holding it out to her as if in a peace offering. One of the leaves fell off and fluttered to the floor. We both reached down to retrieve it. We would have banged heads had we been anywhere near the same height. Instead, her hair caught on the top button of her shirt—the shirt I was wearing.

This only became obvious when I straightened up first. Or tried to. Huguette was not as tall as the button. She screeched and pulled back, dropping the lettuce leaf she'd won. She yanked her scalp and me in the direction of the galley sink with another yelp. She bumped up against it, scratching at her head.

I was apologizing and trying to pull the strands of her hair out of the button holes while keeping a grip on the massive lettuce. "I'm so sorry."

Something in French.

"The button. . . ."

Something else.

"Your hair. . . . "

I had a feeling those weren't words I'd learn in a text book. I had almost freed the last, captive hair when Huguette slipped a bit and sent us both against the sink. The impact yanked off the button and pulled another from its hole. The lettuce head went flying.

There was an entombing silence. I heard the lettuce land somewhere. I couldn't bear to look at Huguette's face. I heard someone approach and turned to find Chance in the entrance, frozen in mid-stride, an inexplicable expression on his face. I glanced down at myself and saw the top half of my shirt gaping open. I grabbed at fabric and folded it around myself, jumping back and bumping into the counter. Only then did I look at Huguette.

She had raised both hands to the crown of her head and stood erect as if facing a firing squad. No, that was the look of the squad itself.

I felt a different kind of anxiety rise. The bees had nothing on Huguette.

Chance was still standing there. I opened my mouth, and Huguette's arms exploded from her head.

Chance and I jumped. She made a look of disgust at no one in particular and stormed out of the galley, brushing against her son and pivoting at a perfect right angle in the direction of her cabin.

I looked at Chance and repeated myself. "The button . . . her hair. . . ."

I saw him trying not to laugh. His diaphragm was already pulsing, and he not only bit his lip, he sucked half of it between his teeth. Then he gave up, and I found myself also doubled over in hilarity. The laughter I'd been trying to suppress surged from my stomach, from some almost-forgotten place. It was deep and unstoppable.

Chance was the first to recover. "*Maman* . . . you. The looks on your faces!"

He started laughing again. I hadn't stopped. I moved toward him in the odd magnetism of two mirths seeking to merge. In so doing, I slipped on the lettuce leaf and lost hold of my shirt.

CHAPTER 18

I plunged forward onto Chance. He caught me by the shoulders. I pulled frantically at the green-and-white fabric and backed into Gilbert. He was standing in the galley entrance.

He was swathed in netting and lit by the soft light bouncing off the water and through the window. He smiled, "So all is OK? *Bien.*" With that he followed the direction his wife had taken. After a few seconds, I heard a door open to the loud sounds of Huguette. The door closed and the sounds muffled.

Chance was trying not to laugh again.

I pointed at the floor. "The lettuce. . . ."

". . . will need to be washed before it becomes a salad, yes?" He started to bend over, checked to make sure I hadn't also, and picked up the dented head of lettuce and the smear of a leaf I'd tripped on.

"I should apologize to your mother."

I moved to leave, but Chance shook his head and

let out a sigh as he thumped the lettuce on the counter. "No, no. It's better for her pride if you act as though nothing happened."

A door opened and then shut with less ferocity than earlier. Quick little steps headed back in our direction. Huguette made straight for the miniscule laundry area across from the galley where I could see my washed clothes through the glass of a front-load washer. She grasped a basket, stepped down with it, and walked over to me while poking her finger inside. By the time she reached me, she was holding three safety pins most matter-of-factly in front of her nose. Then she pointed them toward a green stripe and held them out. I reached for them, still clenching the top of my shirt together.

She snapped her head forward and back two inches. Before I thought to say "thank you," she was gone. Her footsteps sounded up the wheelhouse stairs and out onto the deck.

I was left standing with fabric in one hand and pins in the other. I pocketed the pins and backed out of the galley. "I think I'll go fix this and then hang my laundry. No offense to your mother, but I can't wait to get out of her clothes."

Chance came to the galley door and paused with a grin. "I don't know. I think I'll miss the shirt."

Back in my cabin, I assessed the damage. Though

the shirt opened almost to my navel, there was so much fabric it probably hadn't revealed much.

I patted the shirt down, aligning the button holes with their buttons. Or the one button. Two were gone, and one hung by a thread. I reached in my pocket for the pins. I was ramming the last pin in when it met fast with flesh.

I started crying on the spot.

I sat down on the hard bed, hands in fists. I thumped the mattress on either side of me. I squeezed my eyes closed and saw my trip so far: the baggage track shaking to a stop in Paris. The bees in the back of the Renault in night rain. The awakening to smoke. The airborne lettuce.

The contractions of crying shifted, and, before I knew it, I was laughing. I felt on the verge of mild insanity.

There was a knock on the door. "Melissa?"

I sat up and smeared tears across my face. "Yes?"

Chance continued, "We are all dining together for dinner tonight. I hung out your laundry. I did a bad job, but with a breeze everything should dry soon. Do you need anything?"

"No. Thank you."

"My pleasure. I will see you this evening. *Au revoir.*"

"*Au revoir.*"

I washed my face in the miniscule sink, losing the sliver of soap down the drain and getting water everywhere. When I stood up, I narrowly avoided grazing my forehead on the mirror. Somehow, I felt the impact of it anyway.

"No, that's for hands. *This* is for dishes."

Mr. Once gave me a hard kiss to the forehead and lifted the soap dispenser from my hands in a wide arc, as if to emphasis the order of the well-planned granite kitchen: the cupboards without handles, the stainless steel appliances, and the special cleansers to keep them all free of streaks.

I washed my plate with the approved soap. When I looked up, he had already left the room.

He would be in front of one screen or another. The television screen to watch a game, the computer screen to buy some new gadget online, or the back-door screen to look out over his lawn. If he was at the door, he would notice the flattened rectangle of grass where I'd laid a towel (the wrong towel) to catch a brief ray of sun.

I found him in front of the computer screen, scrolling through a selection of lawn furniture. He didn't look up, but pointed at an Adirondack chair. "What do you think of this style?"

"I think that wood must be endangered to cost so much. Is that the price for a single chair?"

He looked up at me, and it was the let's-not-have-this-discussion-again look.

I held up my hands. "It will look great, I'm sure."

"I wonder if four is too many. Maybe two and a

bench?"

"Maybe I'll leave you to your shopping and head home."

"Sure, sure."

"I was joking."

"*Hmm?* No, that's actually a good idea." He stretched back. "I've got an early morning, and you had a long day. Thanks for picking up the pizza." He stood up and gave me a quick hug. "Want me to walk you to your car?"

I looked into those blue eyes and tried to see his soul. Instead, I saw a kaleidoscope of push and pull. Right now, I had a feeling he would genuinely prefer to order chairs.

"I found a spot right out front, remember? But thanks. Don't stay up too late at that thing."

"*Mmm-hmm.*" He was already sitting back down.

CHAPTER 19

On deck, the bees were flying. Every day, they left their hives for distant places. They turned what they found into something sweet. Perhaps I needed to take a lesson.

"Everything is all right?" Gilbert asked.

"Yes. Everything is all right. And I would like to help."

"*Oc.*" He turned toward the aft stacks of boxes. I followed. He paused at a carton jumbled full of nettings and hats. He pulled out a hat and reached up to set it on my head. I bowed, accepting the odd coronation of plastic pith helmet hung with fine netting. He then disentangled a long, once-white jacket from another carton. He shook it out and extended it toward me, looking at what was left in the box. I took the jacket and slipped it on, snapping the front closed. When I was done, Gilbert was holding out a pair of black gloves.

But he didn't hand them to me yet. Pointing to his own hat and netting, he made stuffing motions with his hands near his collar. I did as he showed, tucking in the bits of net.

He handed me the gloves with their extended wrist lengths. I was now all covered except for my lower calves. Gilbert looked at the bare stretch of my legs. *"Moment."* He turned back into the wheelhouse.

Huguette appeared from amid the bee boxes, carrying the smoker used earlier in the morning. She also wore a white jacket. She came over to me and tucked the sleeves of my coat into the wrists of the gloves. "The bees do not like the smell of us." She lifted an arm, sniffed her armpit, then shook her head. "They no like. Also no *parfum.*"

Gilbert reappeared as she finished adjusting my coat collar. He held a very long cotton sock from each hand. *"Bien?"*

"Bien," I said, trying to smile. *Distract yourself.* I accepted the socks and sat down on a deck chair. Gilbert and Huguette had turned toward the bees. Neither of them wore gloves. In fact, the only protective covering they wore consisted of the netted hats and light white jackets.

Huguette was not using the cardboard rolls this morning. The smoker she lit was a metal cylinder not quite a foot tall. It was set into a cage-like base attached to a bellows. She alternately added twigs and stoked it with a poker. Gilbert approached and began pumping the bellows. Thick, white smoke puffed up from the opening.

Gilbert gestured for me to come a bit closer. Huguette positioned the smoker near the entrance hole to a bee box at deck level. Gilbert approached the box from the side, watching the exit patterns of the bees for a few seconds before going nearer. Huguette pumped several puffs off smoke near the hole.

Gilbert explained, "We let the guard bees know we are here." He was pointing to a gathering of bees near the slit that opened along the bottom of the box. The box itself looked like a single, rectangular, filing cabinet with a lid. The front and back were narrower than the longer sides, and all had a handle indentation.

The bees were noticing our presence.

I started to itch under the jacket.

Gilbert lifted one lid while Huguette aimed a few puffs of the white smoke inside. "We wait half minute. It is good to visit during nice day like this. Worker bees are in the fields."

I coughed. "This morning you said the smoke calms them. Why?"

Huguette answered, "They think there is fire. Bees like to make hives in hollow trees."

Hollow trees. A buzzing started in my head as she continued to pump the smoker.

"They smell smoke and think the forest burns. They . . ." she flapped her arms in a fanning motion ". . . to keep home cool."

The hazy gray smoke made my eyes water. I blinked fast, trying to see clearly, and the sound in my head became an odor. *Hollow trees.* I could smell the rotting bark of a memory and something else. Something like the pheromones Shirley Temple of Doom gave off when Aunt Tifi's neighbor's dog got out of its yard.

Fear.

I was sweating and smelling of fear. I was sure the bees could smell it, too.

So I ran.

CHAPTER 20

The angel came again. The one without feathers. The one who'd first come when I finally left Mr. Once.

The angel's wings were made of stars. A soft down lined his back and the nape of his neck—the only parts of him I saw. Sometimes, I caught a hint of fierce profile when he started to turn and speak. But he kept his head forward, his outline softened in the silvery light. I recognized him as a guardian, facing what might come.

Only once had I seen his face. One night, not long after The End, I had cried myself to a dank and frightening frenzy. Curled on the floor, I had slammed my eyes shut, and there was the angel—so close his features were blurred. He held my head in his hands, whispered my name, and said, "Everything will be all right."

I had not seen him since he'd turned to face me. He came now. I saw only the rise of his shoulder blade lifting and contracting the length of his wing. Stars loosened from him and grew, filling the space between us with a bright light.

❖

The light did not come from stars. It was the late afternoon sun hovering low in the sky. I focused. I was wearing a beekeeper's garb, sitting on the grassy bank of the canal. The barge was invisible behind a curve of green. I paid close attention to each of these details as I looked at the netted hat upside down a few feet away. My back was stiff.

How long had I been sitting here?

Since I ran from what I remembered. It had been ages since that childhood memory of the hollow tree had surfaced. I didn't know what would happen if it fully emerged here. In this place, I already seemed to be shifting my sense of self.

I stood up, pulled off the gloves, picked up the hat, and walked back through the trees. The high grasses waved in the winking light.

Back at the barge, only bees were on deck. They were quiet and contained. I stood on the gangplank and watched several of them making ellipses in the air. They glowed in the sunlight, appearing larger than they were. I stepped past the shadow cast by the wheelhouse to the stern where my laundry was waving at me in the breeze. My clothes were dry and stiff. I unpinned them and draped them over my arm.

When I descended into the barge, Huguette was emerging from the galley. She looked at me, blinked a few times, and said, "Dinner is soon. You come for this?"

I nodded.

She headed for the master cabin at the stern. I was relieved at the lack of commentary or question. If this was the pride-maintenance I'd witnessed earlier, I was fine with it. I went to my cabin, holding my clean laundry close. It smelled like strange detergent and sunshine.

My clothes. I had never been so glad to see my own clothing. I dressed in my travel outfit, thinking that the last time I had pulled on these pants, I had been in Illinois and had no idea I would be living with bees.

At the thought of them, my mouth went dry. I licked my lips and noticed they were chapped. I'd probably sat in the sun too long. I leaned toward the miniscule mirror and almost choked. My normally pale skin was bright pink. I put my hands to my face as if I could rub it off. "No! No, no, no." My lips seemed to catch on each other.

I fished around in my purse for the lip balm that lived somewhere at the bottom. The contents were a complete jumble.

I dumped my purse out on the bed. Wallet. Passport. Water bottle. Keys. Mixed nuts. Compact. Nail file. Baggage claim—keep that out and remember to call. Flight itinerary. . . . What was that? It was an envelope I didn't recognize. I turned it over. No markings. I opened it with the nail file. The card was plain. No salutation, no signature. Just four words: *The angel came, featherless.*

My spine actually tingled. I turned the card over and looked for some sign of its sender. I read the line again and then returned the card to its envelope. It must have fallen from one of the books Aunt Tifi gave me. Even so, I couldn't remember ever having told her about the recurring dream. Maybe I'd forgotten.

I had almost forgotten the sunburn. I pulled out my thankfully large sunglasses and fluffed my hair in front of my face. Checking in the compact, I told myself it was marginally better. Maybe a bit of powder everywhere but the cheeks. . . ? I snapped the compact shut. Why bother? This was my first night out in France, and I was the color of lobster.

Scraping sounded from the deck above. I left my room. Gilbert appeared in the galley when I did. He looked at me with more concern than his wife had. "Were you stung, Mel?"

"No. I'm—I'm sorry I ran off." I felt my face redden further as I pictured what I must have looked like in flight. "Where are we going for dinner?"

He tilted his head and turned, curling his finger to have me follow him. I ascended the stairs after him, trying not to trip in the dim light coming through my dark sunglasses.

As we crossed the gangplank, he said, "Ah, *c'est bon* all the family together. For to celebrate, tonight, we go on a long journey to the best restaurant in town."

Huguette appeared and cackled—there was no better word for it. "So far away, that if we criticize the cooking of Emil from here, he will hear us and put garlic in our *kir*. Come."

She led the way toward the restaurant extending from the lock. From the lower level of the canal where the barge was moored, most of the restaurant and mill were visible. But as we approached, I noticed that the large and leafy hedges hid an outdoor terrace right along the water.

The mill wheel turned so slowly as to be almost silent, lifting mercurial water into the evening light. Large balls of pollen wafted from the plane trees and landed further along on the placid canal water.

It was so lovely, I slipped up my sunglasses to see it without interference.

But there was still interference. I could hear the brothers talking in heated tones even before Gilbert announced, *"Chance et Blaise sont là."*

CHAPTER 21

The brothers were indeed there, facing each other over flutes of a red drink and deep conversation. Two candle flames sparred between them in the last of the evening light. Their table was one of several extending from a low, wrought-iron fence hung with planters of red geraniums. An enormous artichoke had grown through the fence gate, anchoring it open in confident spikes that cast pointed shadows toward us. A brown dog lay on the pavement, lifting just its tail at our approach.

Chance saw us and rose, looking relieved. Blaise, his back to us, turned slightly and took one last puff on his cigarette before stubbing it fiercely out.

As we approached the table, Blaise remained seated. He pointed at me, "You should wear a hat. You are as red as a. . . ."

"Lobster, yes. I noticed." I glared at him.

Chance tried not to smile. Gilbert did, but patted

me on the back and led me to the seat at the head of the table facing the canal, the brothers at my right and left. Gilbert and Huguette sat across from each other at the end nearest the canal.

The remainder of sunlight reached across the water, sending eddies of reflections circling under our chins. As if on cue, we all turned our eyes to the last sip of sun being swallowed by the trees.

The waitress, dressed in tight jeans and a loose blouse, interrupted the reverie with a tray of olives and the same rosy drinks the brothers had half finished.

"Kir cassis," Blaise explained, thanking the waitress and lifting his glass.

"And *olives du pays.* Our regional olives." Chance tapped the bowl. "Emil will serve us a special menu. Do you mind?"

I smiled. "It would be a pleasure."

Gilbert raised his flute of *kir cassis,* and everyone did the same. He looked at his boys who were avoiding each other's gaze. "To family." He looked at me, "from near and far." He looked at Huguette. "And to my wife. We celebrate our fortieth *anniversaire* this year. She is still the reason for my heart and the heart of my reason."

Huguette reached across the table, pushing at his shoulder and pretending annoyance at the flattery. But I saw her meet her husband's eyes.

We all clicked rims. My glass met Chance's, my eyes met his.

He smiled, "Well done."

"Well done, what?"

"You made eye contact during the toast."

"It might come as a surprise, but I have a few social skills."

After the olives were almost gone, Blaise drained his *kir* and leaned back in his metal chair. He tapped me on the shoulder and pointed to the field visible between the trees. "Today, you can see the *douce France.*"

Chance leaned forward, "I told her of it this afternoon."

"But did you sing the song?"

Chance leaned back, waving his hands. "Oh no. I leave it to you.

Blaise declined, "No, to Gilbert. *Papa!* You are the *chanteur, n'est-ce-pas?*"

Gilbert dipped his chin to his collar and smiled. "I sing."

I wasn't sure if he meant he *could* sing or *would* sing. Someone giggled. I think it was me. My glass of *kir* was half empty and my stomach was entirely empty.

Gilbert lifted his chin. "I will sing Tifi's favorite Trenet song." This statement brought a round of cheers. I reached for the second-to-last olive, hoping the food would come soon. Gilbert cleared his throat and focused on the sky.

La mer
Qu'on voit danser le long des golfes clairs

A des reflets d'argent
La mer
Des reflets changeants
Sous la pluie

The entire table joined in. I knew the rhythm but not the words. It was Tifi's favorite Darin song, "Beyond the Sea." But apparently, Darin got it from a Frenchman.

I sang along in English, humming when I forgot a word.

More diners arrived mid-song and took the table behind us along the fence. They applauded when the song ended. Gilbert turned and gave a quick bow from the torso.

Huguette said, "Trenet was a great singer. The last troubadour."

I looked up. "Chance mentioned this is the land of the troubadours."

Gilbert nodded. "Trenet was born in Narbonne— not so many kilometers from here. Also a canal town."

Blaise exhaled the last of his cigarette. The smoke curled up and suspended above him. "Trenet once said, 'I make songs like an apple tree makes apples. They come from inside of me.'"

From inside of me came a growl. As if she'd heard my stomach, the waitress appeared with another tray. Thank goodness, food. I'd missed lunch. I looked up and was surprised to see two bottles of wine instead. The waitress poured Blaise a test splash. He approved and indicated he would pour. She said something in laughter, swatted his shoulder, and disappeared with the tray.

A solo olive sat fat in the bowl. My head felt like it was turning to feathers. I wanted to lean over and kiss Chance.

I what? I brushed my hand over my head to keep the feathers from lifting away. That's what you get for having angels without feathers. You end up with them floating everywhere else.

Huguette's end of the table was speaking French. Blaise was explaining the wine to me. "It is *vin du pays d'Oc—Domaine de la Roque.*" He reached for my glass.

"Just a little." I handed it to him.

He poured me a full glass and did so for the rest of the table before lifting his own. "To the business of brothers." He gave his brother a measured look that was met with a concentrated blankness.

Right then, the bread and starter arrived. *"Macaronnade de foie gras de canard et sa confiture d'oignons.* Like an onion chutney," Chance explained.

Reaching for a piece of bread, I said, "What is this 'business of brothers?'"

Huguette made a sound. "It is the business of disagreement."

Gilbert looked at his sons. "Sweetness and light." The non sequitur hung gently in the evening air with the sounds of conversation from other tables.

Chance cleared his throat and Blaise rolled his eyes.

Gilbert continued, pointing at me, "In your

language, Jonathan Swift wrote a fable. A bee breaks a spider's web—he is trying to escape. They start arguing. Who is better? Spider says: bee is worth nothing—he has no property. Bee says: spider's web is just dirt. Who is better?"

He was looking at me. "I'm guessing 'bee' is the right answer."

Gilbert nods. "The bee fills his hives with honey and wax, sweetness and light. He is content with no things. Just flight and language. It is not a worry, personal ownership." He leaned closer. "It is important this sweetness and light."

Somewhere beyond the fuzz of the *kir* and wine, I remembered an essay. "Didn't Matthew Arnold write about this?"

Chance took a sip, "Yes. He popularized it. He said sweetness is beauty. Light is intelligence. Any good person, or society, is the result of both."

Blaise finished his wine with a scowl. "Say sweetness, say light. I don't care. I want to renovate the mill, to build a real distillery. It's bad enough I must work the lock. But also he," he pointed at Chance, "wants instead to expand the restaurant."

"You know I've wanted to do this for years. It would support the *Honigschlecker*—menus featuring the local honey. The tourists would love it."

"What, they would not like my mead?"

Chance set down his glass. "That is not the point. We want to bring people here, to this village. We need people to support the stores, the *Coopérative*, the. . . ."

At this, Blaise quietly slammed his fist on the table and started a tirade in French.

Without looking at his son, Gilbert reached over, grabbed his fist, and whispered. Blaise immediately slunk back and locked his jaw.

It seemed so obvious, I couldn't resist asking, "Why can't you do both?"

Huguette gave me a look the equivalent of a stop light, but I ran it.

"Seriously. This place is huge. Why not do both, but link the restaurant and distillery with a *pension* where people can stay? Working tourism. People stay and pay to help work in the distillery, they eat at the restaurant, shop in the village. The start of it all is the *Honigschlecker*. Your bees are the heart of it."

I looked around the table. The brothers were staring at each other. Huguette was staring at Gilbert. Gilbert was smiling at me. "I think this is a good thought. We will talk on this, yes?"

I took a sip of the red wine. "In fact, if you ever need any help with the English marketing, I have far too much experience."

Chance raised his glass to me. "I, for one, accept the offer."

Life was just shifting to perfection when the waitress reappeared with plates of snails.

CHAPTER 22

Huguette slapped the table and said Emil's name in pleasure.

"Escargot?" I asked, choking a bit on the "g." Or maybe on my wine. My wine glass was still full, though I had a feeling someone had been refilling it. I focused on the snails. "How do you get them out?"

Huguette pointed to me and then her plate. "Watch." She picked up a thin, wooden skewer in one hand and a blackish shell in the other. She held the skewer lightly and poked inside the shell. The pointed tip caught the body of the snail and lifted it out. *"Voilà."* She pinched off one end and held it up, shaking her head at me and saying, *"La crotte."*

"Huguette," Chance set his skewer down and shook his head at his mother.

She shrugged and said in English, "What, why is it wrong to warn not to eat the shit?"

Blaise laughed, "Why, indeed?"

I reached for a snail and its bowels. Gilbert was dipping his *escargot* into the garlic butter sauce and gesturing for me to do the same. Everyone happily plucked, pinched, and dipped.

I poked my skewer randomly into the spiral opening. It slid around, eventually lodging on the flesh of the thing.

"I got it out," I said aloud. Chance leaned over and pointed out the end. I pinched it off.

He smiled, "Your first?"

"Isn't it obvious?"

"Don't worry, once it's in the butter, you'll love it."

I took a swig of wine, leaving greasy fingerprints on the bowl of the glass. "Here I go." I dipped the *escargot* into the butter and popped it into my mouth, starting to chew before stopping to taste it. I swallowed.

When I looked up, everyone was watching me with curiosity. "It is . . . good."

"That is what God said when he finished creation." Gilbert popped a dripping bit into his mouth.

They *were* good, though I had a feeling it was mostly the garlic butter sauce. I started on my second. "Where do you, um, find them?"

"We get ours from the garden," Huguette said.

"Tifi loves to garden. I've never tried. What do you grow?"

"Many things. Tomorrow you can help in the garden. Maybe better for you than the bees, eh?"

Blaise lifted his skewer at me. "Yes, maybe you practice your 'working tourism,' *hmm?*"

116

I was glad I'd never met Blaise when *he* was a teenager.

❖

As the sky darkened, the candles grew brighter, shaking shadows across the linen and dishes. The wine in my glass cast a red glow in the shape of a heart on the white table cloth. I was smiling at it when someone splashed more wine inside. My eyebrows lifted, and I started to protest, but Blaise continued to divest the bottle of its contents.

The *cassoulet* arrived and Chance pointed to it. "Now this is true *cassoulet*. Only in France would a gastronomic council meet to decree that *cassoulet* must be seventy percent beans. . . ."

Blaise interrupted, "But the other thirty percent varies. So long as it's made in this region, it is *cassoulet.*"

Conversation was becoming increasingly French, and I was becoming increasingly aware of the wine. Too late, I realized that if I stopped drinking it, Blaise would stop refilling my glass. The *cassoulet* became a bit of a blur, correct percentage or not.

Eventually the cheese plate arrived, but things remained foggy until dessert—at which point I had become beautiful, charming, and proficient in French. Everyone else seemed to think so too. I licked my fork, poking myself in the tongue. I returned the utensil with great precision to my plate.

I couldn't tell what language Huguette was

speaking to Chance. Frenglish, maybe. I pretended to understand, nodding when anyone else did.

At one point, a short, busy-looking man came out in a white apron, hailing the table. Emile introduced himself to me and asked everyone how the food had been. After a while, Emile seemed to morph into the waitress. She held a tray of espresso cups.

Hallelujah.

I didn't even wait for everyone to get their cup. I took a deep swig, used to hot, to-go coffee. It took about three seconds for me to discern that this wasn't just coffee. I almost choked.

Blaise smacked me between my shoulder blades. "Ah, you did not know there is water of life inside?"

"Water . . . *cough* . . . of life?" I could feel my sunburned face blossoming.

Blaise took a shallow sip of his coffee and then explained, "This drink is called the *cafine*. It is coffee with very strong liquor, *eau de vie*. This was made by Uncle Jean-Luc. He distilled for years and taught me. We still have a few of his bottles on the *Honigschlecker*.

Chance frowned at his brother. "Not so many left."

Blaise tightened up and retaliated in French. Chance, quiet but barbed, shot back. Without a further word, Blaise heaved himself from his chair and stalked off the terrace.

CHAPTER 23

Blaise's abrupt departure ended the dinner. The family began to scoot their chairs from the table and move away. I did the same, focusing on my feet and marveling at how I could feel each rib of fabric in my socks. These French chairs were complicated. Someone took my arm. I followed the hand up to find it belonged to Chance.

"This way up."

My aunt and uncle had already turned back toward the barge, close in conversation. I accepted Chance's hand and turned to follow them.

Then I stopped short, running into Chance. "Wait." I stood still. He waited.

I held up a finger. "I forgot to call my mother. Is there a phone?" I looked around. All the other customers were gone. I even looked up, maybe for telephone wires. The stars were thick and bright.

Chance tried steering me forward, "Maybe

tomorrow is better."

I stood stock still. "Nope. I promised. If I don't call, she'll send out the dogs."

He laughed, "What?"

I leaned back until my heels rocked. "It's an esspression."

Chance pulled me to vertical again. *"Hmm.* A walk might be good for you. There's a phone booth at the harbor." He steered me toward the lock bridge.

"My mother worries about me. I finally took a vacation. She's watering the borage." I extended my hand to illustrate the height of the borage, but it went more horizontal than vertical. I smacked my hand into the bridge railing. "Ouch."

"Watch out for the architecture," Chance said with a grin. "How long is your vacation?"

"It's dark down there." I leaned to look down into the gaping hole of the lock, and Chance firmly took my arm.

"I only get ten days of vacation a year."

"That has always amazed me, your tiny American vacations. And what about the *bourragé?"*

He said it with a French accent, and I tried to imitate. *"Boo-raaaah-jehhhh.* It's the vowels. You do funny things with vowels here."

"Or I could say you do funny things with vowels there."

We were walking up the tow path. A few lamp posts mingled with the trees, giving enough light to make the dark seem darker. The canal sat black and still.

I released my arm and walked around Chance to be farther away from it.

"What are you doing?"

"I don't want to fall in. I'd have to borrow your mother's clothes again."

He laughed. I stubbed my toe on something and decided to focus on walking.

We reached the harbor, its surface stippled with light. Chance said, "We're here."

"Where?"

"At the phone booth." He pointed to a bright, glass box beneath a tree. I crossed my eyes in an attempt to get them to focus on the blue handset.

"Where do I do funny things with vowels?"

"You're sure you want to call your mother?"

"Yep." I pulled open the door, walked into part of it, and then shimmied in. I opened my purse and studied its contents in the fluorescent light. Wallet. I pulled it out and held it up.

Chance gave me the thumbs up and said, "I'll wait. Take your time."

I returned the gesture and caught my hand on the metal phone cord. After inserting my credit card upside down and wrong side in, I finally dialed and started singing *"Alouette, gentille Alouette . . .* Hello? Mom? It's me! I'm in France!"

"Melissa? I would hope so. Why didn't you call yesterday? I've been worried."

"I'm in France!"

"You said as much. What have you been doing?"

"Living with bees and drinking water."

"Or drinking something."

"Water. Water of life."

"Melissa."

"Do you remember the French cousins?" I looked out the phone booth and saw Chance half a block down the street, looking at a window display. I slunk against the phone and let my head rest against the top of it. "Uncle Jean-Luc's nephews help out with the honey business."

"The what? Hello? You said something about. . . ."

"Melissa is going to work with bees. On a barge."

"A what? You're breaking up."

"A barge. Aunt Huguette and Uncle Gilbert live on a barge. Did you know that?"

"You can't charge what?" Static. "Do you need . . . 'oney?"

I held the phone out at arm's length and shook it. I spoke slowly into the receiver. "No, I don't need honey, they make it."

"Melissa . . . hear you . . . bad . . . 'nnection."

I shook the phone again and this time it banged against the side of the booth. I looked into the mouthpiece as if something were plugging it. "Mom?" Nope. There was pure static on the other end. I sighed, alternately looking at the blue receiver and holding it to my ear until Chance appeared at the door.

"No dogs now?"

I held out the phone, "Bad connection. She thinks I need honey."

He took the hand piece from me and stepped just inside the booth, reaching over my arm to return it to its hook. "Maybe you do."

He stood still for two, full seconds before he stepped back and bowed with a sweep of his arm. He held it aloft as I curtseyed and exited the booth, closing my purse.

Chance bent his extended arm and offered it to me as we walked back along the canal. The solidness of his arm felt comforting. I tried matching my steps with his.

I was looking down at my feet when he laughed. "It's harder when you try."

My head came up, "Try what?"

"See, now we've matched pace. It helps that our legs are the same length." They were. He maybe had an inch on me in height, but it was torso.

The alcohol still pumped through my blood, but I had a feeling that the warmth in my cheeks wasn't entirely from a bottle or the earlier sun. We walked back in silence. When we reached the lock house, Chance looked up at the dark windows.

"Is Blaise OK?" I asked.

Chance shrugged.

The coffee part of the *cafine* started to kick in.

We crossed the lock bridge to the lighted shore. I followed Chance to the *Honigshlecker's* plank. The playfulness had waned, though he tried to act as if it had not.

He smiled. "I have seen you to the boat, *Mademoiselle.*"

"Thank you for a lovely evening."

"My family's pleasure. I will stop by tomorrow around ten if you would like to go into town. I have a friend with a lovely boutique. I am sure you would like her clothing." He stood there, looking at me.

I lifted a hand to my mouth. "Don't tell me I've had parsley in my eye teeth all night."

"No, no," he pulled my hand away and kept it. "Not at all. I was just thinking you look much better in this shirt than in my mother's after all. Goodnight, Melissa." He brought my hand to his lips and kissed it.

"Goodnight, Chance." I turned and walked on board, back erect, taking the straightest steps I could. At the door, I turned back to wave. He was still there, hands in pockets. Light from the stained-glass angel stretched across the bank and onto his face. When I opened the wheelhouse door, plain yellow light absorbed the rest of him. He waved and disappeared.

CHAPTER 24

I slept like the stones at the bottom of a swift river. When I woke, my tongue felt chalky and almost as numb as when I'd drunk the *eau de vie*.

Oh, the *eau*. I lay still for a few moments before gauging what would happen if I moved a limb. I prayed the please-no-hangover prayer. Then I shifted from my side to my back, and the motion didn't send any fault lines cracking through my head. I sat up. Slowly.

I brought my feet to the floor and decided I was fine. Then I stood up too fast. And sat promptly right back down. Real water. I hovered toward the bathroom and tried dipping my head down to the sink to drink from the faucet.

Someone knocked on the door. "Melissa?"

It was Chance.

"Yes?" I croaked. What time was it?

"Did you want a bit more time?"

I scrambled soundlessly for my purse. My watch

said quarter past ten. I hopped one-legged into my pants, "Five minutes. I'll be right up. Shall I meet you on deck?" I fell onto the bed with a thud.

Chance, with a smile in his voice, said, "That's fine. Take your time." I heard him retreat down the hall.

I was struggling to button up my shirt when I realized it was inside out. I yanked it off and pulled it on the right way, buttoning furiously. I swiveled back to the bathroom. I tousled my hair and tried a smile.

I looked awful. How could I be pale *and* sunburned at the same time?

I stuck my tongue out at my reflection, crammed my feet into my shoes, and ran out the door.

Why was I rushing? We had spent three hours on dinner last night. No one was going to die if I was a few minutes late. How would Catherine Deneuve make her entrance? I gathered myself together and did my best to glide past the galley. I took each stair carefully up into the wheelhouse, glad I didn't have much of a headache. The sunlight pierced through the stained glass. The inside of the angel was too bright to look at. I donned my sunglasses. They were fast becoming my most useful travel accessory. And they made me feel a bit more Deneuve.

I opened the door to find Chance on deck talking with his parents. The sun fought a dark knot of clouds. They took turns winning.

Chance turned to me. He looked like he'd been asleep by nine and had already had a jog along the canal followed by a vitamin shake. He winked, "Slept well?"

Huguette and Gilbert, topped with netted helmets, greeted me good morning. I assumed we could skip the kissing since it would mean contending with the fabric around their faces. I was wrong. After getting a mouthful of netting, I stepped back from Gilbert and noticed he looked a little pale around the edges, too. But he put on a crinkly smile, "We let you sleep in. Good idea, no?"

"Yes. I feel spoiled. Sleep in and then go shopping."

Huguette shook her netting and it billowed about her neck. "Good thing, too. Your bag? Gone. Those thieves in Paris." She turned and kicked up her heel in disdain and began mixing something in a bucket.

Gilbert shook his head, "If you have the number for baggage claim, I am glad to call for you."

I opened my purse. "That would be wonderful. Oh, I left it in my room. I'll get it."

Chance pointed to shore, "I'll be at the car."

Gilbert started priming the smoker as I headed back into the wheelhouse and below deck. I turned toward the galley and then stopped, peering toward Huguette and Gilbert's cabin. The door was open.

No sounds came above from the wheelhouse. I heard thumping from the prow deck. I turned and tiptoed toward the door, peeking in at the double bed that looked more like an American-sized twin squashed to a square. Their cabin was wider than mine; no hallway shaved off a side of it, and it took up the width of the stern. Checking over my shoulder, I stepped into the room and peeked around the door. A little bathroom boasted a shrunken tub, tiled from floor to ceiling in a soft pink with a line of black running around the middle and behind the sink.

Across from the bathroom, a secretary desk stood, its cover opened out as a writing surface. On it were neat stacks of letters and papers. A large book lay open at the front. I stepped closer and saw it was a kind of ledger. Maybe for the bees?

"Silly," I whispered to myself. Even if I discovered some marvelous family secret, I couldn't understand it. I turned to go, but caught a familiar name on the top letter. Aunt Tifi.

I started to reach for it just as I heard a noise above deck and spun around. I raced toward the salon and my hallway beyond, reaching my room in seconds.

I found my baggage claim and climbed up the stairs without glancing back.

"Here you go," I said to Gilbert, handing him the baggage claim barcode and the card Max had given me.

"*Bien*. I call."

"*Merci*. And about the bees . . . I'd like to try again."

He patted me on the arm, "Of course."

On the bank, Chance was waiting in a rusty Citroën. He started the ignition, and a soft female voice came on the radio as he turned around in the courtyard and started up the drive.

I pointed at the radio. "Your language is lovely. Someone once told me a Frenchman could read a phone book and make it sound romantic. I think it's true."

"It is beautiful. Though sometimes I wonder if French is my original language."

"How do you mean?"

"I thought my first language was bees."

CHAPTER 25

Chance merged onto the road. His words dangled in the air alongside the cross hanging from the rearview mirror.

I finally asked, "Your first language was *bees?*"

"When my grandparents died, I was very young. When a beekeeper dies, you must tell the bees he has gone, or they will die with him. It is called the 'telling of the bees.' They did this at the funeral, and it made an impression on me. *Mon père* said afterward I thought I was a bee. *Ma mère* said I'd have to be a drone because the worker bees were females." He laughed, "I didn't care. I hummed until I was five. That summer, your Aunt Tifi came to visit for the first time. She had just married Uncle Jean-Luc."

This surprised me. "That was the first time she met the family?"

He nodded. "No one even knew they had married. No one knew they were coming. It was a hot and windy

August day. I was on deck, barefoot and shirtless, 'helping' my father. He was gathering honey, and I was trying to fly. I turned to see Uncle Jean-Luc helping a woman across the plank. She wore a long dress the color of pale acacia honey. The dress had layers and layers of fabric floating in the air."

"I remember that dress." I said it so softly the engine drowned my words. Chance continued without hearing me.

"Grandfather had told me about the queen bees. Tifi was the queen. I believed hers must be the language of bees. My first actual word was English, though I didn't know it."

I felt a tingling at the back of my head where the headrest would be if it hadn't fallen off. Time seemed to pause, even as the landscape unfolded outside. I remembered Tifi wearing that dress to my kindergarten graduation. It was the first time she had given me *The Little Prince*. I had sat in her lap as she read it to me, thinking how lonely the Prince must have been to have only a rose for company.

The road paralleled the canal and its trees again. One minute the banks were so close, you could see the blades of grass curving to water. The next minute, you veered away at a right angle, and in seconds the line of plane trees stretched, distant, along vineyards and villages, and you felt as if you'd left a friend. The next time the canal appeared, her banks might be low stone walls, shallow like curbs, or deep harbor lining.

However varied the shoreline, the plane trees were

a constant. I imagined their long roots braiding beneath the canal with their neighbors on the other shore, just as the branches often did above-ground, arching over the waters.

We passed through fields and vineyards in comfortable silence, though it wasn't so much silence as wordlessness. The car rattled, and the passenger visor flapped like a gull's wing.

I remembered riding next to Mr. Once in his leathered Audi, all sounds of road kept thickly out. But even with every detail designed just for comfort, a rough silence had sat between us, tangible as the separate temperatures we could set for driver and passenger spaces. When I reached over into his air with my words or body, I disturbed his careful climate. I sensed that if I was to reach over to Chance's side, he would not call it his own at all.

It was time to let Mr. Once go—once and for all.

A crop of red poppies shook along the road's shoulder as the first drops of rain pelted the car. Recalling Chance's last statement, I asked, "What was your first word?"

He smiled, "Honey."

I laughed. "It figures. Too bad honey requires bees."

A sloping vineyard rose and sunk past us like a wave. Sun broke a cloud open, and young vines turned translucent in a brief green sea. Chance turned to look at me. "What are you running from?"

I crossed my ankles on the bare metal floorboards,

pressing my heels together until the bones hurt. "I'm not running *from,* I'm running *to.* An adventure, something different."

Chance looked at me long enough to make me nervous about oncoming traffic. He finally faced forward again. "I ask because I wish someone had asked me before I ran off once."

"Ran off where?"

"To Oregon, the States."

"Ah. There was more involved than farming. What were *you* running away from?"

"A woman." He accelerated into a curve. "I should have stayed." He paused and smiled. "So that is why I have permission to tell you what to do. That, and I am French."

Outside the windows, the flattening plane of land stretched across the fogging windshield. Chance flicked on the wipers. I was wondering about the woman when I noticed a castle rising in the south. It was a walled fortress larger than three of my neighborhoods back home. I pointed, "What town is that?"

"Carcassonne. The medieval part on the hill is the *Cité.* We'll be in the modern town below."

We passed old buildings stacked next to each other like books on a crowded shelf. Their roofs blended together in centuries of settling, smeared across with red tiles. The castle disappeared as we entered the edge of the city.

It was stranger for me to be in a foreign city than a foreign countryside. In the country, I expected strangeness. In the city, I expected familiarity, and so the differences were magnified. Long, yellow license plates. Low street lights on roadsides. Cellulite ads with great lengths of naked legs.

Chance pulled into a parking lot and fit the Citroën into an empty space. The hum of the engine ticked into stillness. Rain gathered force. I started to calculate what time it was in Chicago but decided I didn't want to know.

I followed Chance out of the car and across the lot toward a line of buildings broken by a narrow street. He glanced at his watch. "There is still time before the lunch pause. My friend's boutique is in the *Place Carnot.*"

The one-way street boasted no sidewalk, just metal railings spaced out about three feet from the craggy gray walls. I walked behind Chance, wanting to stop and look at everything—at the butcher's and the chocolatier's. Even the shoe repair shop. I was a tourist who felt like she wasn't supposed to get excited about a cobbler hammering a heel onto leather shoes. But I did. As I turned to catch up with Chance, I almost ran into him. He had stopped at a corner where our street fed into a city square. Hard rain started falling through tall, skinny trees onto a bustling vegetable market. Tarps and awnings flapped in the wind as vendors secured them. I held up a hand to shield my eyes from the sharp downpour.

Chance came close to my ear. "You see that little café, *Le Petit Moka?*"

"Yes."

"Across from it is Sophie's boutique." He waited for me to locate it. I scanned across the Neptune fountain rising from the market. The god was getting drenched and was probably glad of it. I spotted the boutique beyond him and nodded.

"Shall we run for it?" I asked.

Chance looked mischievous. "Shall we race?"

"What does the winner get?"

"Coffee after."

"Deal. Ready, set, GO!"

CHAPTER 26

An hour later, I stepped out of the boutique into bright noon. The sun was polishing rain-washed streets and cars and lampposts.

I was happy, and that was a pleasant change. I stood still, feeling my new clothes against my skin. I glanced across the full square toward the café where Chance had gone to wait for me. He owed me a coffee.

The market square sprawled between us. A squat old woman in a headscarf lifted a bunch of beets high over her head. She aimed them and several words at a round vendor. He wiggled the small, square blackboard sitting in the rest of his vegetables and patted the chalked price. The number "1" resembled an upside-down "V." The woman waggled beets again. The man scratched his second chin and shrugged. He reached for a pink bag and held it to the woman, looking away as she stuffed her purchase inside.

The boutique door opened behind me. Sophie

came to stand next to me in front of her window display. She asked, "You know where are you going?"

I turned. "Yes, thank you. Just enjoying the sunshine. You live in a beautiful place."

She crossed her arms and took a deep breath of the spring air. "*Oui.* Have you seen our *chateau*, you call castle." She nodded behind her in what I guessed to be the direction of the fortress we had seen from the road.

I shifted my bags. "The castle on the hill? I was hoping Chance would have time to show me that."

She turned her folded arms to me and looked down at my new pants, a mid-weight linen with doubled seams and generous pockets. I'd chosen them with the thought of staying on a barge. Yet even in their practicality they possessed a style and stitching my other pair lacked. Sophie looked up at my face. "You looking more better. More better, yes. You know Chance good?"

"No, we just met. We're sort of related by marriage."

"Ah, I see." She licked her glossy, full lips and tilted them toward the sun, still keeping an eye on me. I set my bags down. My old clothes, wet from the rain, were weighty.

Sophie looked me full in the eyes, "He is engage with my sister. Secret." She held a well-manicured finger to her lips and made a soft *shhh* sound.

I couldn't tell if I was more surprised at the news or the sudden vacuum that hollowed a spot below my sternum. I kept my eyes on hers, wondering what my face was doing. I looked across the square again. What had been full of promise inverted into a familiar ache.

Sophie was watching me. I tried a smile. "You must be so excited. Are you helping her find a dress?"

Sophie looked at me for a beat and then mirrored my smile. "She is designer, you know this? She design many of the clothes I sell here. She even make the lovely dress you liked."

I turned to the window display behind me. A creamy concoction hung from a headless mannequin in soft folds. It looked like the dress Chance and I remembered Aunt Tifi wearing.

Sophie was still smiling. "My sister is good, no?"

"Marvelous." My voice was flat.

Sophie turned and scanned her windows, finding a fingerprint. She rubbed at it with her sleeve. "She also sell at other places. Paris and Marseille. Look for the label 'Mado.' It is like her name but. . . ."

"A nickname."

"*Oui*. Nickname for Madeleine."

The name hovered in the air. I glanced at my watch. "I'd better go." I picked up my bags with one hand and extended the other to Sophie. "Thank you so much for your help. And the discount."

She leaned forward and kissed my cheeks instead of taking my hand. She pointed to my new clothes. "Same if you come again. Special friend price."

I walked into the square wondering if Sophie's discount had been a bribe or if sophisticated French women could tell you to stay away from a man in one breath and then offer you special retail rates in another. If so, I didn't want to be sophisticated.

I didn't really care about Sophie, but I had to work at not caring about Chance. He had said and done nothing to suggest he felt more than kindly toward me. *Kindly.*

The label in my collar suddenly itched. I wanted to pull off my shirt. I felt like Mado was strangling me.

At the edge of the market, just beyond a cheese stall, I saw the two layers of outdoor tables at *Le Petit Moka*. Chance sat at the outer layer lining the cobblestone street. Behind and in front of each table sat two wicker chairs, side-by-side. Chance faced the square, or rather the newspaper he held in front of him did. I crossed the street behind a delivery van and came up beside him.

The newspaper shook. "Mel!" He stood and took my bags. I started to sit.

He held up his hand, "Wait, turn around. I want to see the full effect."

I circled slowly and took the chair he offered.

"You look lovely, Melissa. And you have won a *café au lait*. I must say, I was glad to lose."

My earlier happiness had evaporated like the rain. I thought of Chance putting a flower behind my ear yesterday, and I felt my ears burning—this time with irritation.

Chance swiveled and gestured through the glass window. A man with narrow hips and wide hair appeared shortly after. Chance ordered our coffees. The waiter nodded and asked me something.

Chance translated, "Anything else? A snack before lunch?"

"No, thank you." But I hadn't had breakfast and my stomach reminded me of this with a growl. Chance smiled and spoke to the waiter who acknowledged the order and turned on his heel.

I found myself trying to juggle hungers and finally decided the physical one would be the easiest to manage.

Chance caught me staring in the direction of the boutique. "I think you will feel better after some food. You have never been to this country. You cannot pretend you do not want to try the famous pastries."

I was only partly listening to him. I was thinking of his future sister-in-law across the market.

Chance sighed theatrically. *"Mais non,* you cannot be one of these obsessed American girls who count every calorie? Or what fad was it? The one where you do eat bread or don't? Where you have all fat or none?"

Before I had a chance to answer, the waiter reappeared holding a tray with our coffees and two pastries.

Chance pointed to each of them. *"Pain au chocolat* and croissant. But first. . . ." He rustled in one of the bags under his chair. He emerged with a small paper box and lifted it forward in two hands. "A special treat. We start with a bit of savory."

Setting the box on the table, he lifted off the top and pulled out two more pastries. These were of a denser crust than their sweet neighbors and resembled fat spools of thread with a miniature pie-crust pinching around the tops.

My irritation was dissolving at the sight of food— to my further irritation. "What are they?"

"Petits pâtés. Usually they are made with roast mutton, sugar and lemon zest." He held one up. "But I like them with one modification." He extended the *pâté* to me. "Guess what it is."

Curious despite myself, I took a bite. A rainbow of flavors hit my tongue. The *pâté* was sweet and savory. Brightened by the lemon, the edge of the mutton was sweetened with. . . .

"Honey?"

"Très bien. I convinced a local baker to use our honey instead of sugar."

I took another bite, trying to hate him.

I failed.

I had to admit it—if only to myself: I had hoped. Chance had been my first source of hope in a long while. And perhaps I was mourning the loss of that even more than him. I almost laughed at my silly self.

Chance saw my smile. "And?"

"It's wonderful. I can see why you want to take over the restaurant."

He leaned forward, "I already have a menu in my head. Honey roasted lamb, honey drizzled over small rounds of *chèvre.* I think my veins run with honey. Ah *miel.*"

He tilted his head. "You know, your name sounds

a bit like the French word for honey."

That could be a romantic line under different circumstances. I wiped my hand with the flimsy bit of napkin and saw Sophie's lip gloss forming the word "sister."

I took a sip of my café. "You still have to pick up the netting for Huguette. Do we need to go?"

Chance leaned back in his chair, interlacing his fingers behind his head. "Let's enjoy this sunshine first."

I broke off an end of the *pain au chocolat* and sent flakes across the plate and table. It was hard to be angry while eating chocolate.

A young woman walked by with a cigarette. I watched her disappear into a street past an old building on the corner. Its dark brown shutters matched the chocolate I licked from my fingers. I asked Chance, "Do people live above these shops?"

"Yes, I think so. Although not so many also work below. Not like it used to be." He followed my gaze to the building.

A shadow crossed near one of the second-story windows. An old woman came to stand near the glass and look toward the café. She pressed two eager fingers against the window pane as if in blessing or recognition. But she did not see what or who she sought because she turned with a sad face and disappeared into the dark interior.

Chance had seen her too. "Do you ever imagine the stories of people behind such windows?"

"I live in a large apartment building, and I only know names from the mail slots. Well, maybe one woman by face. We say 'hello' when she takes her dog for a walk."

I could feel Chance watching me. "Let's try it," he said.

"Try what?"

"Try imagining this old woman's story."

I felt a surge of competitiveness. I was already ahead. "OK. You start."

"The woman is a widow. Her husband died in the war, and she had been so passionately in love, she never desired to remarry. Just this morning, over breakfast, as she takes a bite, she has a clear memory of him eating his croissant fifty years ago." Chance took a bite of the croissant. A few flakes sifted from his lips. "This memory was so clear she thinks he was waiting just outside to come in with the newspaper. She rises and goes to the window. . . ." Chance handed me the croissant.

I took it and looked back up at the window, thinking of those two fingers that had pressed there. I wondered if she had left prints on the glass. I bit into the pastry and thought for a moment. "She goes to the window and looks down to the street, expecting older cars and younger friends. But no one stands at the door waiting to be buzzed up. She glances across to the café and sees the old man sitting alone watching the sky." I nodded in the direction of an old man sitting at the last table. "For a full second she thinks it is he—her husband who never came back from the front. They never found his body, and she had always hoped. She looks closer. . . ."

For a second, I had forgotten where I was and with whom. I set the croissant down, but Chance didn't pick it up.

He looked at me. "She looks closer and sees it is not her husband. But for just a moment she doesn't care. She wants only to be held. . . ."

I'd had enough. I pushed back my chair. "She gets her binoculars and can see he's wearing a wedding ring. So she lets the curtain fall back into place. The story's over, shall we go?"

CHAPTER 27

The Citroën curved around a Van Gogh copse of cypresses and pulled to a stop in front of a stone cottage. It was surrounded by fruit trees. Flowers grew on and out of everything.

I noticed these details with the same enthusiasm I had mustered to write descriptions for boxed wine.

As we climbed out of the car, a man appeared around the side of the house, netting tucked from a beekeeper's hat into his collar. He waved a big glove in our direction and yelled something friendly.

Chance waved back. "Jacques!"

Jacques pulled off his hat and netting to greet us. He dropped them and his gloves near the farmhouse stoop, a stone rectangle that centuries of feet had worn into a shallow bowl. The thin oval of rainwater pooled there had already begun evaporating in the afternoon sun.

"Enchanté," Jacques told me, shaking my hand. I

was beginning to guess that one kissed hello only with family or established friends.

"Enchanté," I repeated.

Chance nodded at his friend. "Jacques doesn't speak much English, so I can translate whatever I wish."

Jacques' tanned forehead crinkled as he turned from Chance to me and back. He spoke, pointing behind him to a stable building.

Chance turned to me, "Do you want to come?"

"No, thanks. I'll wait here."

The air was fragrant with flowers and the bees pollinating them. I watched a single bee climbing across a petal. The flower gave her pollen. The bee accepted it.

I walked around the grounds, smelling flowers, running my hand on the bark of trees I didn't know by name. I couldn't seem to think about anything, but the walking helped. I had gone up and down the drive when I heard a woman's voice.

"You are Melissa?"

I looked up to see a very pregnant woman standing barefoot on the stoop, wiggling her toes in the water and smiling.

I smiled back. "Yes, hello."

She gestured toward a bench beneath a window and sat down with a heavy sigh. "The baby is very soon to come. I wanted to meet you. *Oooph.*" She rubbed a hand over her broad belly, and then extended it to me. "I am Michelle."

"You have a lovely home, Michelle."

She looked around her, nodding. "Lovely, yes, but too old. Me? I like a house with central heating, walls that don't fall down." She turned her flushed face to me. "How long are you staying with Huguette and Gilbert?"

"Ten days."

"What? You come all the way here and only stay ten days? Stay longer. You can come visit me. I need to use my English."

I laughed. I liked the instant ease of this woman. "I would like that, but aren't you going to be rather busy with a baby?"

"Never too busy for friends." She looked in the direction the men had gone earlier. "You and Chance—you are friends?"

I gave her my best blank look. "Yes. Cousins, really."

"Hmmph. Only by marriage. That is different."

"Yes, well, marriage—or at least an impending one—seems to be a bit of an obstacle."

Michelle looked puzzled, and before she could reply, Chance and Jacques appeared around the corner of the house, Chance with a roll of netting over his shoulder.

Chance hailed Michelle, set down his bundle, and came over to lean his head against her belly. They spoke and laughed in French, and I found myself wanting to learn the language.

Even without understanding Jacques, I could translate his body language. He clearly didn't think

Michelle should be out and was already lifting her to her feet. She was laughing and ignoring him. Chance stood back and indicated we would leave.

I turned to Michelle, "It was such a pleasure meeting you. And you, Jacques."

Jacques nodded, waved at Chance, and pulled his laughing wife inside. The two of them disappeared, and Chance hoisted the netting and tilted it toward the car. "Gilbert told me to get you lunch. Jacques and Michelle would normally invite us, but the doctor told her bed rest." He opened the back of the car, tossed in the netting, and pulled out a cloth shopping bag and a bottle of wine. "So how about a *pique-nique?*"

"You already have everything."

"While you were shopping, I was shopping." He flung a red blanket over one arm like a waiter's towel, and he held the bag aloft. *"Voilà."*

I had no idea what to make of this man. I stood there, silent, until Chance nodded and started off between the trees.

CHAPTER 28

Twenty minutes and several bramble scratches later, I couldn't resist asking, "Where are we going?"

"Almost there," Chance called back. He was six paces ahead on the path, the red blanket trailing him like a cape. I had at least convinced him to let me carry the wine.

We ascended a plateau. Chance's pace slowed to a stop. "This is it." He handed me the bag and flipped the blanket onto a grassy bank. We stood at the edge of a lake ringed by trees.

"It is beautiful."

Chance pulled out a combination knife and flipped out the corkscrew. I handed him the bottle of wine and we sat on the blanket. As he started working out the cork, he said, "Since today is story day, I will tell you the story of the lake. And I am very good at telling this story. When I was home from university in summers, I was a tour guide on the leisure *péniches*. The ones that charge you tourists too much money to float the canal at four miles per hour."

"I may be a tourist, but I probably couldn't afford to charter a barge."

"Neither I. But giving tours was close." The cork *thwopped* out of the bottle. The gentle glug-glug of wine filled the plastic cups and the spring afternoon.

We raised our cups and Chance said, "To Pierre-Paul Riquet, *Santé.*"

"*Santé.*" I looked away quickly this time.

Chance rolled down to his side, propped up by one elbow.

I barely tasted my wine before anchoring the cup in the grass and leaving it there. After last night, I was in no mood for alcohol. "Who's Pierre?"

"Pierre. Yes, everybody likes to call historical figures by their first name. You feel *connected*. Pierre is the seventeenth-century man who had the vision for the Canal du Midi. Ah, Pierre and his Black Mountains."

Chance pulled out wrapped cheeses: a circle, a triangle, and a square. He nodded across the geometry of our luncheon to the mountains in the distance. "Pierre brought a water diviner to the mountainside north of Villefrance-de-Lauragay and Carcassonne. There he discovered the source for his canal. The starting point. On this plateau of Naurouze was a small stream. It divided into two tributaries."

I started lifting up the shapes one by one to sniff them. Chance continued watching the distance, "One

150

went southwest toward the Sea," he lifted his cup in that direction and took a sip. "The other west toward the Atlantic Ocean." He repeated his gesture and then lay back on an elbow while I started unwrapping the mysterious and heady-scented shapes.

"Pierre decided to build a reservoir to supply water. He built this *Saint-Ferréol Bassin* in 1667. It was the largest artificial reservoir in the world. Pierre financed everything. Every inch dug with a shovel."

I tore off the tempting end of baguette. Taking Chance's pocket knife, I spread one of the least strong of the cheeses on it. I took a tentative bite. Quite good.

I remained upright, kicking off my shoes but hugging my knees to my chest, reminding myself this was not a romantic picnic. A few fat clouds rolled far above the water's surface, reflecting themselves there.

Chance continued. "This reservoir feeds the canal which goes 145 miles between Toulouse and Sète and has 63 locks. . . . I bore you. I will stop with facts."

I said nothing, and he rolled over onto his back, resting his wine on his chest. I rose toward the sandy beach of the water's edge. A stone wall banked the shore not far away. I stood and walked toward a cluster of rocks breaking through the sand. The sand was the color of my office cubicle back home. Home. When I thought about that word, I wondered. Home wasn't my apartment. It wasn't my mother's house in the suburbs. It wasn't Aunt Tifi's. It wasn't here, with a man someone else would make a home with.

I heard the sound of splashing and turned to see

Chance, his pant cuffs rolled up, standing in the water.

"You are very serious this afternoon," he told me.

"When Aunt Tifi wrote, she said she wanted me to join her in France. But I suspect she never meant to meet me. She just wanted to get me on a plane and away."

Chance touched my elbow. "Come. I want to show you something."

He led me along the lake to a stream. Further into the trees, we came to where the stream rushed from the earth, raucous and loud. He pointed. "Doesn't it look like the setting for a myth?"

It was an idyllic little cove formed of rocks, trees, and water where creatures from legends and the heavens might appear at any moment. But I didn't want to agree with him. I remembered something I'd read once. "Myth's ancient meaning is that which was true, that which is true, and that which will be true."

I stepped closer to the water and balanced on a large stone. The water in front of me coursed up from the earth. I wondered at its source below.

Once I was sure of my footing, I added, "I want truth."

Just as Chance opened his mouth to respond, a geyser shot from the rocks and spit spray toward sky. It was an instant white column of force and noise. When it faded, the shock and water left us at the same instant.

I turned to look at Chance, slightly behind and above me on the rocks. He was laughing and shaking off water like a dog.

I started to shake off water, too, but I was standing on a sloping, now-slippery stone. I lost my footing and slid sideways. I would have landed on a jagged rock had Chance not grabbed my waist. He used more force than my weight required, and I found myself held close to his torso. And very, very conscious of it.

We stood eye to eye. Our rapid breaths came and went with different frequency. He slowly loosened his grip and then stopped.

Before I noticed the distance between us, his mouth was a breath away from mine. He took my top lip gently in both of his, holding it a beat and then doing the same to my lower lip. My mouth parted from instinct and from the intent to say something. But instinct won, and I forgot he was engaged. Or I remembered to forget.

And then I kissed him back.

CHAPTER 29

Around the time I felt his hand on the small of my back, the reality of the rocks, water, and kiss landed in some rational part of my mind. I shivered and placed a hand on his chest. I felt the indentation of his breastbone.

I had just enough time to register the question in his eyes before I pushed away from him. His eyes widened in surprise as I lost my balance and fell backward into the stream.

The water folded over my front as I submerged. I saw Chance crouched in the failed save but didn't see the details of his face. I closed my eyes, mouth, and nose. Time slowed. I opened my eyes and saw a galaxy of bubbles rushing up to the surface. I saw the skin around my bicep flowing like fabric.

What was seconds spread into a full shimmering moment. My life did not flash before my eyes, but a small, past part of it blossomed and froze—the first time Mr. Once had kissed me. In this underwater reliving, it turned into the last kiss. I let both—and everything in between—continue downstream. I expected a kind of peace. But anger came in its stead.

My head burst the surface right next to Chance's extended arm.

He reached for me as I kept hold of a rock a couple of feet downstream.

"Melissa, are you all right?" His face was tight with worry.

"Fine, fine." I waved his hand away and started to scramble and slip out of the water. My linen pants felt like they weighed pounds and pounds. I wished I had been lifting weights. I tried to heave myself up and hovered over a rock. Chance reached under my arms and heaved me upright. I had an odd sense of déjà vu.

I caught my breath and balance on the rocks, shedding water. Streams of it ran from my scalp into my eyes and ears. He reached a finger out to slide away a chunk of hair that had plastered itself to my cheek.

"No," I brushed his hand away.

"No, what?" He asked, smiling and reaching for my hand to help me back up the bank.

"No to everything." I walked past him toward the path.

I was several yards down the path when I heard him come up behind me, then beside me. When I still hadn't acknowledged him, he spun in front of me and stopped. I almost ran into him. Everything on me was dripping. I wiped at my sleeves and started to ring out my hair.

He scanned me up and down, "You didn't hurt yourself did you?"

"No," I said, wrenching the end of my twirled hair. Water landed on the path with a splat. "Shall we go back and get our things? I'd like to return to the barge and shower."

He smiled. "You can't get much cleaner than bathing in that water." He leaned closer, "And you look lovely when. . . ."

"Chance, I can't," I held up the hand still dripping from my hair. "I. . . ." I didn't meet his eyes, but looked around him to the path. "Can we go?"

I started past him, but he grabbed my elbow. "What is wrong? Don't be embarrassed about falling in the water."

I yanked my elbow out of his hand and looked at him, my anger crystallizing into a hard knot. It swelled red into my head. "You don't have the right to tell me what or what not to do. And you especially don't have the right to kiss me." I waved him away and walked forward for the third time.

For the third time he stopped me. This time with his own anger. "The right? What are you talking about? If I remember correctly, you kissed me back."

I shook off his arm with force. "Stop pulling at me." I tried to douse the anger. "Look, it was a mutual mistake. Let's just forget it and go back, please."

His face hardened. "It wasn't a mistake for me." This time he turned first and started back toward the lake.

What had just happened? *Had* it happened?

I had started to do what Mr. Once had done to me. Which left me without the superiority that had helped me survive that failure. All my judgments of him? Cancelled with a willing kiss.

I tried to forget the kiss. It was like trying to forget the universe. With Chance, I had been the woman with sunlight on her lips.

I turned my mouth from the sun and followed the path back.

CHAPTER 30

The returning drive was drenched in tension. This time, the silence felt electric, and Chance dealt with it by cranking up the radio the minute he started the ignition. Like brother, like brother.

And when we returned to the barge, I felt like I was stuck in some strange replay; here I was again on the bank of the canal with a *Honigschlecker* brother, soggy inside and out.

The other brother was standing outside the mill with Huguette, looking at the foundation.

Chance handed me my things from the back seat. We stood facing each other. I could feel the damp ends of my hair soaking the dry shirt I'd changed into. This was ridiculous.

"I'm sorry. . . ."

"I shouldn't. . . ."

We spoke simultaneously but found no humor in it. Chance just nodded, gave me a tight smile, and turned toward the mill.

So that was that.

I sighed and turned toward the barge. In the salon, Gilbert was sitting at the table with a stack of papers. He looked up and asked, "Did it rain hard in Carcassone?"

"You could say that. Did you have a good morning?"

"*Oc, oc.* I am dreaming." He pointed to the large papers in front of him and gestured for me to come closer.

Spread out in front of him was a brittle width of unrolled parchment with an architectural plan marked on it in faded brown ink.

He patted the drawings. "The mill. It needs much work."

I sat down and looked at the lacy script describing rooms and measurements.

Gilbert ran a finger to the section showing the second story. "Here would be good view for tourists, no?"

I saw a twinkle in his eye and asked, "A *pension?*"

"Huguette thinks these are bad places. But I think your idea, this 'working tourism' is good. Huguette likes people to work for her." The twinkle turned into a smile.

Just then, Huguette stomped in.

She saw me and looked closer. "You have new clothes! From Sophie's? Oh, she has such lovely clothes *n'est-ce pas?*"

I sighed. I had briefly forgotten Sophie et al. "Yes, it's true."

The new clothes animated Huguette. This surprised me. She was wearing a plaid version of the outfit she'd lent me earlier.

She picked up my bags and pushed Gilbert's plans aside. He rolled his eyes at me and obediently moved to the corner. Huguette slid the clothes across the surface and they unfolded to a stop. All the wet ones just thumped in a ball. She gave me a sharp stare. "What happened?"

I sighed. "It was raining. Hard."

Gilbert was trying not to smile. "Melissa. I called about your bags. . . ."

Huguette nodded. "No news. Like I said, thieves. Oh, this is good." She held up my splurge. I had eyed Mado's creation in the boutique window but couldn't justify the euros for it. This was more pragmatic anyway. A versatile splurge.

Huguette nodded again. "Yes, you could even look good in this."

I decided her pronouncement was a matter of translation and took it as a compliment. "I'm always looking for the perfect, little black dress. This, well, it's not too little, and I can dress it up or down."

"And you can wear it to church."

"Sure. You go to church?"

Gilbert coughed.

Huguette gave me a look for which I, as yet, had no category. It was a look that would drive the devil himself to don his Sunday best.

I was trying to think how to get out of a lecture when I gave up. I reached for my dress. "Well, I'll wear it to church but not in the garden. You said you could use help?"

"*Oc.* I meet you there in a few minutes. I need to talk with him." She pointed a finger at her husband and frowned.

He batted his eyes at his wife, *"Bien sur, Madame."*

CHAPTER 31

Unsure what a "few minutes" meant, I decided to explore within close range of the garden. I left the barge and stood on the bank as the lock started to split open. A modern, white boat sat inside, slowly sinking from the water level upstream to the downstream level. A young man stood at the piling keeping an eye on the boat. The water boiled and frothed, sending surface waves past the *Honigschlecker*. The white boat sat regal and still as if carried on a bier. The water lowered her gently and with perfect distribution. She didn't waver once.

Blaise had complained about running the lock, but I had seen neither brother manning it. It seemed the brothers were lock keepers in name only and probably to appease their mother.

The last of the water rolled out, leaving the lock gates dripping. The craft glided through, her captain hidden behind tinted glass.

I turned up the gravel path toward the large mill building behind the restaurant. A small courtyard connected the two, and a stretch of vacant stables I hadn't noticed before nestled behind both at the base of a low hill.

The mill stood umber and sturdy. I walked around to explore the back of it. The sun had already moved across the canal, and I stood in shade. I shivered and picked my way through the high grass toward the nearest window. Half a shutter hung from one corner, and I could barely see up over its sill. As I came near, I could hear voices. Chance and Blaise. They were arguing. I leaned my back against the rough stone to the side of the window.

The voices grew in strength and speed until one of the men slapped a wall. Or his brother. Silence followed. I held my breath—I could hear them breathing. They must have been standing closer to me than I thought. A chunk of stone wall was boring into my lower back, but I didn't move.

One of the brothers stomped out of the building. The other said something that sounded like a curse and stomped off in the other direction. I was left with no idea which way to retreat without being either seen through the window or from other exits.

I stood still a moment. Had Chance said anything to Blaise about the picnic fiasco? And if so, what did the fight mean? Or was I completely self-absorbed, and they were just fighting over what color to paint the walls?

After waiting a few moments after the last footsteps had receded, I walked across the driveway toward the garden. Both men had disappeared.

The garden had once been surrounded by a wall, but most of the stones had tumbled away and wildflowers were left to grow along them. The earth nearest the canal looked like it had recently been planted. Neat furrows of soil ran parallel to the water.

Blaise appeared from the forest and stomped through the garden path, not seeing me until he was a few yards away. He stopped short.

All I could think to say was, "Good afternoon."

He confirmed it wasn't by grunting and continuing by.

After Blaise disappeared into the mill, Chance emerged from the barge and headed directly for the lock bridge. He crossed to the other shore and headed for the field.

Huguette clambered off the barge seconds later, hailing me to come toward her. "No garden work now. You help Gilbert."

The bees again. I literally squared my shoulders and headed for the barge. I *was* going to do this. "Shall I put on the gear?"

"No, no. Not here. He wants to look for old papers in the lock house." She leveled a stare at me, which was impressive, considering our height differences. I braced for a reprimand. Instead, for the first time, she gave me a genuine compliment. "Your idea last night is good. I think maybe you are the best to help Gilbert until the boys, how you say? Cool out."

I smiled. "It would be a pleasure."

"Good. I hope you are better with paper than bees."

CHAPTER 32

Gilbert and I crossed the canal, its water perfectly still, pollen pirouetting above its surface. No boats approached, and the young lock keeper's assistant was nowhere to be seen.

Of all the family, Gilbert was the easiest to be with. We walked in companionable silence up to the lock house door. He knocked, waited, and shrugged. With a flourish and a bow, he gestured for me to enter.

I stepped into an entry hall. The only open door was to the left. It revealed a bright room dotted with a confusion of furniture. I turned inside. Toward the back near the dining table, an entire wall was covered with shelves.

Thankfully the lock house didn't smell like a bachelor pad. On the contrary, it smelled like an herbalist shop. Lavender, thyme, anise. The scents came from the rows of jars, tins, and cans lining the back shelves.

I walked toward them, fascinated. "It smells like an apothecary in here. Do your sons collect these?"

Gilbert shook his head. "Many have been there long time, when our whole family lived here. The boys don't like to change much."

I scanned the myriad of container shapes and contents. Amid the jars of dried flowers and herbs, there were wooden toys, decks of cards, photos, old ticket stubs, recipes, magazine cutouts, stones. An entire family history diffused in fragrance and flavor. It was touching to see the brothers leave the accumulation of their lives intact.

I picked up a jar with shards of a root inside. When I unscrewed the lid, a whiff of ginger surprised me.

"Would you like *tisane* of *gingembre?*" Gilbert asked, pointing toward the kitchen.

"Do your sons mind? I mean, us being here in their house. . . ."

"We are family." He gave me a soft look that echoed somewhere in my heart. An image of my father, one of the few memories I had of him, transposed itself onto Gilbert's face. What would it have been like to hear him say that? *We are family.* I kept my buried hunger for a father where it safely was and reminded myself I was already an adult.

I handed Gilbert the jar and followed him into the kitchen. It faced the back of the house and overlooked a wild tangle of a garden.

Gilbert set the kettle on the gas stove and put a few pieces of dried ginger in a chipped, white tea pot.

"While we wait, I show you something." He led me outside to an overgrown terrace with crooked chairs and cigarette butts scattered across its flagstones. Beyond it spread a trellis of pink roses looking like a schoolyard of children let out to recess.

Gilbert took a rose in his hand and smelled deeply of it. "Tifi brought these roses on the plane when she came to visit years ago. She hid the roots in her hat."

I smiled. "That sounds about right. She has a thing for hats."

"I am glad you came, Melissa."

I looked at Gilbert and realized I felt it with him: a sense of home. "I am glad, too. I am glad you are my uncle. I miss Uncle Jean-Luc."

He bent and twisted off a rose. "*Oc.* Me too." He looked at the rose he had picked. "He was gone so many years. It is not good to have anger between brothers. I see my sons, and I see myself and Jean-Luc."

He scraped off the thorns. I wanted to know what he and his brother had fought about but knew it was inappropriate to ask. I only hoped they had resolved it before Uncle Jean-Luc's death.

He handed me the rose and pointed to the top of the lock house. "We explore. Many old things up there I want you to see."

We turned to go inside. In the kitchen, Gilbert set out two tea cups. He looked around in mock sneakiness and opened a tin. He wagged his eyebrows and set a little shell-shaped cookie on each saucer.

"Madeleines," he said.

The kettle started its shrill finish.

CHAPTER 33

I discovered that an attic tea party is an effective way to ward off the blues. Sitting on an old radio, sipping his ginger *tisane,* Gilbert pointed to objects and boxes. I pulled out daguerreotypes, porcelain dolls, and gilt-spined books while he told me their stories.

Ostensibly, we were looking for old records of the mill, but we were both escaping. I was escaping his son, and he was escaping his wife. Although, I had a feeling his escape allowed him to return to her with his equilibrium restored. They were an odd match, but I sensed they loved each other.

And beyond our dual escapings, I felt we shared an understanding of the quiet spaces no one could enter— spaces others could never understand. The mystery was perfectly acceptable.

"What is this?" I lifted out a battered cardboard pyramid with a hole in the bottom. It had been painted gold, and traces of glitter lines created a sense of stones.

Gilbert chuckled. "Ah, I had forgotten about this. Chance made this hat in school. He was in a play about the seven wonders of the world. He worked so hard on this! But he made one little mistake."

Gilbert reached for it and put it on, turning his head back and forth. "Only three sides."

I laughed and took another sip of my *tisane*. "I can't imagine Chance as a pyramid. An Egyptian, sure. He has that bronzed skin. . . ." I stopped myself. "This is like an antique store up here. Do you have any idea where to find the mill paperwork?"

Gilbert shrugged, sending the pyramid tilting. "Try the big case. No. Near the window."

I popped the latch on a black steamer trunk. Inside was a jumble of boxes and stacks of papers.

"The red box," Gilbert said, finishing his *Madeleine*.

It was a shoe box, heavy with papers. I brought it over to Gilbert who set down his tea and lifted open the box. He was as careful and precise as he had been with the bee boxes.

I was pleased to note that the thought of bees didn't make me shiver.

After lifting out several sheets, Gilbert found what he was looking for. "There. That is for the *architecte*. We are finished."

"You knew where it was all along."

He gave me a marvelously blank look that would have worked if he hadn't been wearing a gold pyramid on his head.

I shook my head. "Tifi has nothing on you. Hats or

otherwise."

❖

When we returned from the lock house, Gilbert and I found Huguette & Sons in the salon at the end of an argument. Huguette turned to her husband and began giving him the benefit of the entire conversation at full volume. I discreetly backed out and left through the wheelhouse.

I hadn't spent much time on the deck of the stern, other than to hang my laundry. A built-in bench curved around the entire back, covered in sun-faded cushions. A wooden table sat off to one side. I sat at the back, partially hidden by the clothes flapping on the line.

In a few minutes, I saw Gilbert exit and set off in the direction of the restaurant. I wondered if he was going to avail himself of Emil's well-stocked bar. I wanted to follow him instead of returning to the fray below, but I had a feeling he wanted solitude.

I sat a while longer, watching the sun slip away. The lovely evening contrasted with the familial tensions. Family. Mine was so small that there wasn't much space for tension. It was me, my mother, and— when the whim suited her—Aunt Tifi. I wondered what it was like to have a brother or sister to fight with? More so, what it was like to have a father? I found myself jealous of Chance and Blaise. They had Gilbert, and they didn't seem to know how blessed they were.

❖

"Melissa?"

"Mom. How did you know it was me?"

"Because I've been thinking about you for the last hour."

"One of those mother-daughter connections, *hmm?*"

"Thankfully they exist. They seem to be more reliable than phone connections."

"Sorry about that. Hey, did you know Aunt Tifi's relatives keep bees? On a barge?

"Yes."

"So that's why you said dad would have been proud of me."

"That and for many other reasons."

"But you didn't tell me. About the bees."

"Would you have gone if I had?"

"That's not the point."

"Well, it was your aunt's idea. Blame her."

"I would if I knew where she was. Did she even plan on coming?"

"Depends on whether we go with her track record or with hope."

"Since when do you use 'hope' and Aunt Tifi in the same thought?"

"Careful there, what would any of us be without hope?"

"I'm sure you're right. You always are. Guess what? I tried the honey."

"And?"

"It was good."

CHAPTER 34

I was awakened the next morning by a knock on my door and a woman's voice saying, *"Petit-déjeuner."*

For a full second, I had no idea where I was or whose voice had said what. I was just beginning to wonder if I knew who *I* was, when everything returned. Barge, Huguette, Melissa.

Melissa was starving. I'd skipped dinner—if there had been any. Instead, I had sat by the canal harbor after calling my mother, watching the barges until dark.

Breakfast was a quiet affair. Gilbert seemed tired. His *petits bâteaux* sunk before he bothered to rescue them with his spoon. He drank the rest of his coffee in silence, clapped his hands and said, "No work today. We rest."

"Rest?" Huguette's English failed her, and she started what I assumed to be a list of what needed doing. Bees seemed only one of many things.

Gilbert held up an age-flecked hand. *"Non."* And

with that, he walked down the hall toward their room and closed the door.

Huguette turned her authority to me. "So. You can help me this morning, yes?"

I held the honey spinner over my bread. "Of course."

"We get some things from the market."

I let the last of the honey slip from the wooden grooves.

Huguette nodded at my plate. "You are liking our honey?"

I smiled. "Yes. Do you know that until I came here, I hadn't eaten honey since I was four? I thought I hated it."

"What is this hate? Hate honey?" Defeat was supplanted by indignation, something my aunt was far happier to maintain. She jabbed a wrinkled finger in the direction of my plate. "This is good for you. And it taste good."

She swept Gilbert's crumbs with one hand into another and dumped them on his plate. She told me, "You eat honey here. You work with bees here. No more silly. We go to the market."

Back in the saddle, she was.

I followed Huguette from barge to bank. We each had an empty cloth shopping bag hanging from our shoulders.

"Emile!" Huguette's arm shot out, and she waved it at him. He was coming toward the lock bridge from the opposite tow shore, carrying a similar bag. His was bulging.

Still a fair distance away, Huguette began hollering her French hellos and how-are-you's. By the time we all reached the middle of the bridge, they were well into conversation.

Emile wiped a wide hand on the purple and green smudges of his white apron and leaned forward to kiss us both on our cheeks.

"*Bonjour.* You enjoy your meal at the restaurant?"

Thinking of the *cassoulet* and not the *escargot*, I answered, "It was wonderful. I wish I could cook like that."

"Come today, *après-midi.* I show you some secrets." He waved and continued toward the restaurant.

Huguette called out something that made Emile laugh and then signed for me to follow her. We crossed to the other shore and walked to the *Coopérative.* A bell rang like laughter above the door just as the scent of fruit reached my nose. It was another moment of sound turning to a different sense. At this rate, I would start tasting things that were meant to be heard.

The *Coopérative* walls were lined with shelves of preserves and grains. Below them stood tables with vegetables and fruit. One wide, long table ran through the middle of the room. Huguette hailed a woman holding a little box of round, red berries. The women kissed on the cheeks and started talking.

I scanned the shelves built across large windows. Several shelves held honey with the *Honigschlecker* label—the unmistakable little angel from the barge's stained glass perpetually dipping his finger in the pot.

I felt Huguette's finger poking me in the arm. She pulled me over toward the woman. "Long time family friend. Camille is the mother of my boys' friends."

Camille extended her hand and then the berries. *"Groseilles.* You like to try?"

"With pleasure." I chose two. One fell. I tried to catch it and bumped into the onion display. Before I had a chance to pop the berry in my mouth, a mountain of onions avalanched onto the plank floors. Once the worst of the noise had passed, there was just the sound of a few stray onions rolling into far corners of the store.

This sound, I could definitely taste, and it was sour.

"Oh," I breathed. "I am so sorry. I'll pick them up. Do they bruise? I'm so, so sorry."

Camille waived a hand and laughed. "It happen before. Onions strong like their smell." She bent over to pick up three that had rolled to her feet. Huguette simply stood still, hands on hips, looking at me. She finally shook her head and bent over with a great sigh.

Camille started to tell a story. "Huguette, you remember the summer when your boys work here?" Huguette grunted and Camille continued, looking at me though the legs of the long vegetable table. The underbellies of the tables were rough and dusty. The floor certainly was. Camille chuckled and continued.

"Chance and Blaise, they had the job to stack *pêches*—how you say?"

"Peaches?" I guessed.

"*Oc*. Peaches. So soft and fresh. They were, how old? Eight and ten, maybe. Good boys but boys." She paused to stand and stack several escapees.

I hunted the onions that had rolled the farthest.

Camille continued. "The boys started fighting about something. Who remembers what. They had just finished the *pyramide* of lovely peaches when. . . ." She made a breathy sound and flung her arms wide. "All over. And peaches," she shook a finger, "they no strong like onions. They were like *gelée*." She shook her head and sighed.

Huguette nodded. "They still do this. Not with the hands. Now," she tapped her mouth, "all argue. Still fight, but more hurting."

Camille nodded. "Still children, just taller. Same with mine. Worse, maybe."

The last of the mountain restored, we three straightened and Camille smiled. *"Bien."* She turned and gestured for us to follow her past the counter to a back room.

I dusted off my knees and followed Huguette past the ancient register and worn, wooden counter top. The storeroom was stacked with boxes of produce. Stray leaves and bruised fruit lay scattered about like a casual still life.

Camille led us to a stack of boxes near the open door. She said a few words to Huguette and pulled out a head of lettuce. I shuddered. Huguette accepted the leafy greens and pointed them at me over her shoulder. "Melissa likes too." She turned to look at me as if peeking through a keyhole. I think she was smiling.

I reached for the lettuce and smiled. "Of course. In fact, how about I make the salad tonight. I have a wonderful recipe for dressing from Aunt Tifi. She probably got it from you." I smiled, showing all my teeth, and put the lettuce in my market bag.

Huguette's eyes twinkled and she continued to inspect and accept the cucumbers and peppers Camille pulled from the produce boxes.

I was trying to remember what Aunt Tifi put in her dressing. "Do you have lemons?"

Camille shook her head, "Tomorrow we have. Try town store."

"OK. Huguette, is there anything else you need in town?"

Huguette surveyed the contents of our now-bulging bags. I lowered one of the straps of mine so she could see inside. *"Non.* All is enough."

I pulled out my purse and paid Camille before Huguette had a chance to protest. She didn't protest too hard.

As I was closing my wallet, a woman entered the store and called out, *"Maman?"*

Camille set down a handful of cucumbers and went to greet her daughter. *"Cheri!"* She said, kissing then embracing a blur of gentle fabrics and long, shiny hair. The lovely woman greeted Huguette.

Camille turned toward me with her hand on her daughter's back. "Melissa, this is my daughter, Madeleine. We call her Mado."

CHAPTER 35

My bag of vegetables bumped against my hip with each step. I wanted to look back but didn't. Huguette would still be exalting Mado's beautiful dress, Mado's beautiful hair.

It had seemed urgent, after accepting Mado's gracious thanks for buying her clothes at Sophie's boutique, to go get lemons. I hadn't expected Mado to be so . . . nice.

At the harbor, the morning bustle had begun, but I was no longer in the mood for commerce. I walked past the little stores and crossed the bridge into the village. One street in, and all turned quiet and still. An orange cat uncurled itself from a window ledge and stretched down to the ground. It trotted around a corner. I followed it, trying to think of nothing.

One street led to another, and the cat kept on toward its destination, now and then stopping for an urgent bath or a sniff-appraisal of a door mat. We came to a small, sloping square of cobblestones with a fountain in the middle. A church stood at the highest edge of the square. Its steeple praised the blue sky in a shaded silhouette.

The cat disappeared. The only sound came from the dripping fountain.

I neared the church, *Église Saint-Christophe.* The name was carved in the lintel with a date so old, I couldn't make out the century. 1486 or 1586. The oak doors stood massive and dark, stippled with round discs of metal. A smaller, human sized-door, was cut into the larger one. Its lever was polished with use, and the wood around it was brighter where generations of hands had reached for it.

A building to the right shared a wall with the church. Two nuns emerged, nodded to me, and then crossed the courtyard.

I pressed down on the door lever. A squawk of hinges was followed by silence. The sound repeated as the door closed behind me. I was left blinking into cold darkness. I lifted an arm in front of myself and shuffled forward into the dark.

The stained glass acted as a nightlight while my eyes adjusted. Far up above what I could now see was the altar, a curve of window panes let in red, blue, and yellow light. I walked in that direction and bumped into a font.

"Ouch!" I said aloud to the red marble, rubbing my hip. The water surface didn't register the disturbance. It lay so flat, I wondered if there was any water in it at all. Glancing around and seeing no one, I stuck a finger in, and it hit water. I shook it off, belatedly remembering it was meant for crossing one's self.

I could begin to distinguish the little altar niches. Candles burned deep in the recesses of stone. I walked to the front pew facing the main altar.

"Hello, Mel."

Somehow I wasn't surprised. I squinted into the darkness. "Gilbert?"

The walls and pillars took my voice and ricocheted it among themselves, finally letting the sounds sink into the frescoes.

He stood from his seat in the transept facing the nave and came to where I was. He pointed to the pew near me. "That was my father's favorite place."

He sat down and looked ahead. "He liked to look *gerade aus.* That is German for 'straight ahead.'"

I sat down next to him. "I forgot, your father was German, wasn't he?"

Gilbert was quiet a moment. He focused on the stained glass far above him. "Yes. But it is not always so simple, being German, or French—or even American. To explain, I tell you a story."

CHAPTER 36

Gilbert began with a question. "You know of the Alsace?"

It sounded familiar, but I shook my head.

"The Alsace is a region of France with a long history of back and forth, back and forth between France and Germany. The main city is Strasbourg. A woman grows up in this city during French rule. But when she is a young lady, the Germans take power. They make everyone speak German. She has to learn a new language. She marries a German man. They have a boy. He grows up speaking German. No French allowed. Years later, his mother has an *attaque cérébrale*. Cannot remember anything after the Germans took her Alsace. So she forgets her German. Her boy does not speak French. They cannot speak to each other. The doctors say she does not have long to live. For the last months of her life, the boy learns French fast as he can. With her last words, she asks him to help his people have freedom. He promises her this.

"She dies. The boy's father decides to move to Berlin to be with his family. The boy grows up there. Then the war starts. The young man has a plan. He joins the army to fight in France. But he wants to fight for France. He wants to be like a spy."

"A double agent?"

"Just so. He comes back to Strasbourg. He starts working with the *résistance* and lives in fear of his life. One night, before a dangerous assignment, he is walking to meet the other *conspirateurs*. He crosses the *Place de la Cathédrale* when he sees a girl go inside the church. He thinks she is pretty, so he goes inside too. But it is so big, this *cathédrale*. He can't see her in there. Anyway, once he is standing in that quiet place with the candles, he feels his mother's presence. He follows this presence to the front pew and kneels down on the stone. In the front pew, there is no knee rest. But he kneels on the stone until his knees hurt, and then he kneels more. He forgets he is supposed to meet the others. He prays. No one knows what he prays because he never tells.

"That night the Germans come to the meeting place and take the other *résistance* men prisoner. They all die in camps."

Gilbert looked off to the left transept where he had been sitting when I walked in. "The woman, she sits on the side. Her name is Joan—my grandmother. She saw two German soldiers praying in the front row. She did not like the Germans. Of course, she did not know one

186

was a spy and the other an angel."

"An angel. The Honeylicker Angel?"

"No. That is another story. I save it for a different day."

"I enjoy your stories, Gilbert. I think Chance inherited your love of telling them."

Gilbert turned to look at me. "Remember: no one sees a story the same way, so no one tells it the same way."

He rose and patted my shoulder. "I am leaving. Stay and enjoy the *cathédrale*."

He left along the wall between the right transept and the door. When I had entered earlier, I had not been able to see the details of the walls, only darkness. Now I saw a two-story fresco of a man in a medieval, two-dimensional robe of red and white checks. Up in the darkness of the vaulted ceiling, he held a child on his shoulder. Down at eye level, his feet were submerged in water.

A school friend of mine had been Catholic, and I loved to hear of the saints' miracles. She had told me no proof had been found for "Saint" Christopher, protector of travelers, and he had been removed from the official calendar of saints.

"Well, Christopher, is that because you were an angel in disguise?"

I crossed over to him and put my hand where his ankle would be beneath the painted water. I couldn't reach the red-checked robe. Each square was larger than my hand. I leaned back to look up and see his face, now foreshortened but somehow still looking at me, conveying the weight of his burden.

I stepped back, feeling my own familiar burdens. I picked up the lightest of them, the vegetables, and said goodbye to the tall saint.

When I opened the church door, the light was blinding. It was like emerging from a matinee into daylight, where the story you'd just heard dissolved beneath the sun.

CHAPTER 37

How long had it been since Chance and I had entered the town's fruit and vegetable shop together? One day? Two? The same man stood behind a high counter and said nothing when I entered. I chose a few lemons, forgetting what else I needed. Huguette had plenty of spices and herbs. But maybe a little bar of chocolate for now.

I paid for my purchases without exchanging a word with the silent salesman. We each nodded, and then I left. On a whim, I crossed the bridge and walked around to the other side of the harbor.

A little triangular peninsula poked out from the north bank opposite the phone booth. The patch of grass was just big enough for a picnic table and a leafy tree. It looked like a perfect spot to try my chocolate.

I descended the irregular cement stairs to the boardwalk—if it could be called that. It was a piecemeal stratum of stone and brick, made level by years and sediment.

To a bird in the sky, this part of the canal must look like a snake that had swallowed a mouse. The harbor was digesting a bulge of boats. The back of the body and tail extended east toward the lock house and the Sea. The snake's head ducked under the bridge and arched around the north edge of the village, preparing to strike through the vineyards toward Carcassonne.

My chocolate was open by the time I reached the picnic table. But instead of devouring it on the go as I did back home, I decided to wait until I was sitting beneath the tree. I sat facing the boats and snapped my teeth through a square, letting it melt on my tongue.

Bliss.

Between Gilbert's story and the chocolate, I had forgotten about Mado until I saw her walking from the *Coopérative* down the opposite shore.

She was hailing someone in greeting. Walking toward her was Chance. They reached each other and exchanged kisses.

Mado's ensemble was one you could take from a breakfast meeting to a night club by peeling back a few layers. I tried not to think of Chance peeling back the layers. I squeezed my eyes shut. That only made the image worse, so I opened them again.

They had turned in my direction. I ducked like a fugitive behind the tree trunk. What was I doing? I felt like the high school girl with the inescapable crush who wanted to plot her rival's fall.

I peeked back around the tree. A couple passed in

front of Mado and Chance as they walked toward town.

I remembered the shape of Chance's palm on the small of my back the night he had walked me home from the restaurant. It was the gesture I'd waited my life for, inexplicably. Mr. Once had never liked to touch me in public, let alone walk arm in arm. "It makes me feel restricted," he'd said.

Stop. I'd told myself I wasn't going to keep rehashing the past.

Still, I started to shake. I don't know if I was finally shaking off Mr. Once's words or allowing the anger to leave. There in the shade, I felt unlovable, needy, manipulative. All the things I loathed in others. And all the things that kept slinking back when I wasn't looking. Was it only going to get worse? Would I turn into a passive-aggressive eighty-year-old who would yell from her end of the table, "Wouldn't it be nice to have the salt?"

No.

I came out from behind the tree. Mado and Chance were gone, and so was my anger. If I had come to France to get over myself, I was being given plenty of opportunities.

CHAPTER 38

When the chocolate wrappings were empty, I started back toward the barge.

As I neared the restaurant, the air filled with scents of lamb roasting. The front doors were closed, but the doors opening out onto the dining terrace were flung wide to the light. The woman who had served us the other night came outside and lit a cigarette.

I smiled. *"Bonjour."*

She exhaled and smiled with yellow teeth. *"Bonjour."* From there on, I only heard a river of words.

I shook my head, *"Je ne comprende pas.* Sorry. Emile?" I pointed inside.

"Ah, *oui,"* She nodded vigorously and pointed also.

I was beginning to get frustrated with my inability to speak French.

The waitress followed me inside where the smell of lamb intensified. I followed my nose to the kitchen. Emile was standing at a chopping block in front of an electric spit. His arms were dusty with flour as he kneaded an elastic oblong of dough.

"Emile?" The waitress had joined me at the door. She pointed to me with her cigarette.

I smiled at the chef. "I am here to learn some cooking secrets." I glanced at the lamb with apprehension. "But maybe I should start with something easier than that."

"*Mais oui, mademoiselle.* Come." He patted the dough in front of him. I set my bag down on a table near the door and washed my hands before advancing to the work table. The waitress leaned into the door frame and exhaled in the direction of the dining room. Emile glanced up at her cigarette and waved her away, gesturing to the lamb and his nose.

She wagged her hips at him and returned to the terrace, humming a familiar tune. Emile started singing it while stirring a sauce on the stove. "*La mer. . . .*"

The sea again. I drew a curvy line through the dusting of flour to the edge of the table.

Pierre Riquet had thought beyond the sea too. He had thought of the sea from the impossibility of land, and he had dug his way through earth to reach it. Would this restaurant be here had a seventeenth-century man not fought to build this water route? Would Tifi have married the son of barge beekeepers? Would I be dreaming of a Frenchman who loved honey?

Emile ended his song and his sauce and looked at me as if I was a lazy employee. Pointing to the dough and making kneading motions, he said: *"Malaxe!* Go on." He nodded from the stove toward the bulbous mass in front of me. Its amorphous surface was already stretching in a warm rise.

I started pounding at it in slow motion. Emile took the dough from me as I was mid-punch. "You have to cook with love in here." He tapped his heart. "If you bake with *impatience* or *colère*, you make bitter bread. Bread that satisfies only half a man's hunger."

He hefted the dough up to me, and I dropped it with a thud on a patch of flour. The flour sprayed across my front. Emile pointed at a rack with aprons. I dusted off my hands on each other while he pulled a thick, white apron over my head. I was trying to tie it in back and instead dusting my derriere with flour when Emile came behind me to help. He turned me to face him.

But it wasn't Emile. It was Chance. He brought the ties around front and cinched them at my waist.

He was tying on his own apron and greeting Emile before I found my voice again. "Thank you. What are you doing here?"

He gave me the same look Emile had a few moments before. I started kneading dough with emotions that were not going to take the edge off of anybody's hunger.

Chance introduced himself as "Assistant to the Chef."

I looked to Emile for confirmation. He nodded and beamed, "Chance, he is a chef *magnifique*. I want him to take over so I can retire." He turned to Chance. "And hurry, I want to enjoy *la mer* before I am too old!"

"You are going to retire?" I asked. He didn't look to be older than his early fifties.

Emile nodded at this and added. "Chance started working in this kitchen when he was tall enough to see over the table. He will be even better than I."

Chance was hauling a wooden crate of greens from a stack near the door. *"Coopérative"* was painted on the side. He set the box at the far end of the long table and looked at Emile. He said something low in French, and Emile laughed.

Chance started pulling out vegetables I didn't recognize. I couldn't help but ask, "What's that one?" He looked up and held out a bunch of beets. I shook my head, "No, the white bulb with fluffy green."

Emile answered. "Fennel? What? You do not know what this is? Chance, you must educate your friend." He looked at me, "How can you not know this?" He walked around to the growing pile of vegetables and held up a bunch of carrots with a wink.

"I almost forgot they had green tops."

Chance left the vegetables to Emile and started basting the lamb spinning slowly on a spit. Emile was holding up a mass of dusty green curls.

I grimaced. "You can eat that?"

Chance said something in French that sent Emile into peals of laughter. He set the mystery greens down and shook his head.

I crossed my arms in a mock huff. "That's it. I am

going to learn French."

Emile was red, either from the heat of the roasting lamb or from laughter. "Ah. Yes. It is a good idea to learn. You would laugh very much at this man." He leaned across the table, "And you would understand everything he said."

I looked at Chance. "And what would you think about that?"

He looked at me and then addressed Emile, "I think that's not enough to motivate her."

CHAPTER 39

"Blaise, will you teach me French?"

Blaise was chewing on the salad I'd made for dinner.

Chance was absent. He had accepted dinner plans with a friend and had been vague when his mother had asked with whom. After he left, Blaise had been more specific and said something to Huguette involving Mado's name.

Huguette and Gilbert were apparently reconciled and were animatedly disagreeing over something new.

Blaise seemed to be my designated English speaker. He finished chewing and answered, *"Mais oui. When do you want to start?"*

"As soon as possible. Whenever you're free."

"After dinner? *Huit heures. Ici.*"

I knew the number, at least. *"Bien,"* I said with a smile. My first French conversation. All four words of it.

Blaise looked at me. "Anything else the student wants to learn? Anything else she needs?"

I couldn't read his eyes, and I had the feeling that if I could, I would have preferred to remain in ignorance.

"Um, can you pass the salt?"

My teacher was late. I'd have to ask him the word for "late" in French.

Gilbert and Huguette had walked into town for a stroll. The barge was empty but for me and the bees. One of them was circling in the hallway. I tried not to bat at it and ducked toward my aunt and uncle's room. I found myself standing next to the secretary desk and remembering the letter from Tifi.

I really shouldn't.

But I did. I glanced toward the wheelhouse and turned toward the desk. The stacks of paper had shifted. I lifted a few pages from the closest stack, hoping to see Aunt Tifi's spidery handwriting.

Bill. Chart. Aha. The envelope was there. But not the letter. *"Merde."* I had already learned that word, courtesy of Blaise.

I didn't hear him until he was in the doorway. I don't think I had ever jumped so high.

Blaise smirked and pointed at me as if he had discovered a secret. "So now I know why you want to learn French. You want to sneak in other people's private papers, no?"

"No. No, of course not." I set the letter down. "I was trying to escape a bee . . . I was admiring the old desk . . . I saw Tifi's handwriting." And I *had* seen it—the first time I'd been in here.

Blaise sized up the half truth and then asked the bee that had followed him in, "So: truth or lie?"

Brightly, I walked toward the door. "So, French lessons? Do you want to have them inside or out? It's really a lovely evening, and it might be nicer to. . . ."

"Come," he said, turning on his heel in front of me and starting up the wheelhouse stairs.

I followed him up and off the barge. The early moon was rising over a mercurial strip of water. I asked, "Should I get some paper? A pen?"

"No need," he said, not looking back.

We crossed the bridge and passed the lock house and *Coopérative,* heading toward the village. I trotted to come up beside him. We were near the harbor when I asked, "So, do we speak during French lessons? I don't even know the verb 'to talk.' How do you say that?"

"Parler."

"Great. So how do I say. . . ."

"We go somewhere you can listen. That's how children learn, yes? We first listen."

The lights from harbored barges zigzagged across the rippled surface of the darkening water. Blaise nodded to the left. A small tavern announced its presence with a chipped sign. A curtain hung across the middle of the window. Several heads were visible above the curtain rod in a cloud of cigarette smoke.

Inside, old men sat at the brass bar railing, animated. They faced a small television suspended above the bartender who appeared accustomed to being quite literally overlooked by his customers. The front table was packed with what appeared to be an extended family. I was shocked to see a young child in his mother's lap in the middle of all the smoke.

The back half of the bar was hidden by a wall of corrugated, golden plastic circa the 1970s. Blaise pointed to the table behind the tobacco family. I took a seat facing them and started to listen.

One mead later, and I could distinguish a few words with the help of Blaise's translations.

Two meads later, and we had been invited to join the family. I lost all worries of sounding stupid and was simply sounding stupid with glee. I wedged my chair next to a grandfather who kept leaning over and whispering secrets to my shirt that neither it nor I understood. Blaise sat across from me hollering occasional translations across his cigarette. I coughed and repeated. Then someone else would add a phrase, and I'd try repeating it.

I turned down the third mead. I wanted to keep my head—and use the *toilette*. I excused myself and passed the golden plastic wall, finding it far more endearing than when I'd entered. Beyond it stood a pool table with worn green felt. Two people were playing a game. The man was chalking his cue stick and the woman was pointing to the angle of a ball and shaking her head.

They were a lovely couple. I noticed this before I noticed who they were: Chance and Mado, playing pool.

CHAPTER 40

During the three seconds it took me to register their identities, they hadn't noticed me.

I had choices: I could be exquisitely magnanimous and engaging. Or I could be cool and nonchalant. Or I could duck into the ladies' room.

Mado's back was to me and Chance had turned to replace the chalk. I went with Option Number Three and realized my error once inside the bathroom. Now, when I came out, it would be quite obvious I had ignored them on the way in.

As I washed my hands, I looked at myself in the mirror. My hair had loosened from its pony tail. I left it as it was and resisted the urge to apply lip gloss. No reason to.

I peered out the bathroom door toward the pool table. Mado was sitting on the edge of it, holding the cue behind her. She tested her aim at the white ball with a steady back and forth.

Chance's attention was riveted.

My good intentions crumbled. Just as Mado drew back to make her full shot, I pushed the bathroom door open wide. *"Bon soir."*

Chance's head snapped up and his beer sloshed.

The white ball hit the solid red with a perfect click. The red ball angled off the rail and rolled into the corner pocket with a marbly "clink."

Mado uncurled herself from the railing and leaned against the cue stick in an S-curve. She smiled at me and said, *"Bon soir"* as she set her stick back in the rack and leaned toward me to exchange kisses.

Chance just stood there with his glass.

I smiled at him. "I met Mado this morning at her mother's shop."

Mado nodded. "I am happy to be seeing you like my clothes. It is pleasuring to create these things."

Her thick accent was charming and so was she. Chance seemed to think so too. He was still looking at her. When he finally turned back to me, I told him, "Sorry to interrupt your game. I'll just get back to my table."

With that, I smiled, waved, and returned to the front of the bar. I was greeted with a roar of welcome and a further round of French words to learn.

Blaise was halfway through an ancient ballad, and I was declining all beverage offers with the exception of water when Mado came up to the table. She was wearing a jacket and had slung her purse over her shoulder. She goodbye'd the entire table in a single, graceful moment and was out the door before the male half of the table had a chance to sing for her. They sang through the window, instead.

I looked over my shoulder for Chance and almost bumped my nose into his abdomen.

Blaise rose, using the shoulder of the man next to him for support. He waved for Chance to join the table and pointed to the chair next to me. At some point, the woman with the baby had left.

Blaise leaned deeply across the table, nearly knocking over a candle, and said to me, "Chance is not going to own a restaurant. No. And I am not going to own a *distillerie.*"

Chance's face was not so much expressionless as a face attempting to be expressionless.

Blaise continued. "*We* are going to own them together, with a *pension!*" He thumped his fists in rapid succession on the table, gaining the attention of everyone around it. He stood holding the dregs of his drink toward the electric chandelier above us and started to give an elaborate toast in French.

Chance began to translate. "He thanks me for joining him in a worthy enterprise. A union of family and history. A new beginning for the restaurant and for an abandoned building, blind with age. To this business and buildings, we will bring sight and sunlight, hard work and passion. To brothers."

I was impressed. "He *is* a bit of a wordsmith, your brother."

Chance nodded and raised his glass, standing as well. To the table, he said something in a softer, less oratorical voice than Blaise, who translated this time: "He says a blessing to all present who witness family joining together."

Whatever had been said in anger at the mill seemed forgotten or forgiven.

The blessing made me tired. I wondered if it bothered me that neither brother seemed to remember I had suggested the *pension*. I had an immediate desire to be home in bed, asleep. I pretended to understand the ensuing discussion of enterprise, gave up, and pushed my chair back. My chair legs caught on Chance's. "Sorry," I said, as I tried again, standing up.

I angled toward him, trying to extricate myself from the now increasing tangle of legs—human and wooden. The old man was smiling in the direction of my backside. Chance started laughing, "It means you cannot leave. The table is not ready to release you."

His glass was empty, but his eyes were clear and focused. I gave him a quick smile and the old man a swat. That had definitely been a pinch. Blaise burst into an uproar of laughter.

With one final heave, I sent myself and my chair backward, somehow managing to keep both upright. I curtseyed to the crowd.

"*Merci beaucoup pour la . . . le . . .* lesson? *Pour votre compagnie. Merci et au revoir.*"

Chance lifted an eyebrow. "So we are learning French, are we?"

"No, *I* am learning French from your brother." To said brother, I announced, "I have had a lovely lesson in French . . . everything. My head is too full, and I'm tired."

I waved and blew kisses at the table and pushed open the door into the cool, night air. The table burst into song as I departed. Blaise followed me, shrugging into his jacket and taking the side of the path nearest the canal.

We had just cleared the edge of the building, when I heard the bar door open. He didn't call out but just walked up behind us and next to his brother. I was now two people away from the water's edge and this irked me.

Blaise started whistling. That irked me too. Chance said something pleasant to his brother, and I couldn't take it any more. I stopped and sat down at one of the picnic tables past the harbor and faced the black water. The two men stopped and waited.

I didn't look at them. "You two go on ahead. I'd like to sit here for a moment."

Blaise walked over and sat on top of the table. "It is a good night to sit by the canal."

Chance remained standing but set a foot up on the bench.

Blaise tapped a package of cigarettes on his palm and extracted one. When he lit it, the end turned orange like a distant moon. I looked up to see if the moon was still visible. I couldn't find it through the leaves.

Chance walked toward the shore and crouched down. He dipped his hand in and scooped water toward his face. Then he used both hands and tousled his hair. Blaise joined his brother at the water's edge and asked him something.

I stood up quietly and started back the way we had come. Blaise splashed his brother, and they started a tug-of-war. I remembered Camille's story of the peaches. I had not gone ten paces when I heard the unmistakable splash of someone landing in the water. Then laughing. Another splash.

For once, I wasn't the one falling.

I was almost out of earshot by the time I heard them call my name.

CHAPTER 41

I reached the village alone. An occasional street lamp broke the darkness. A few curtains and shutters let out a yellow glow.

I found myself back at the town square in front of the church. The fountain had been turned off and was now a reflecting pond for the great clock. The clock said it was well past everyone's bed time.

The convent windows were dark but for a single window high to the right. What sister sat there, sleepless? I wondered if she worried about relationships with fellow sisters or whether she only had to work on her relationship with God.

I approached the church and tested the brass lever in the small, inset door. It opened. I was beginning to appreciate small-town living. I let the door close as quietly as it would.

Entering from the night, I could better see the church interior. A few of the chapels still glowed with candles, both electric and flame.

I headed straight for the front row where I'd sat with Gilbert. A few thin, square cushions lay scattered across the pew. I lined them up and stretched out. The ceiling was as black as night sky without stars.

I looked toward Saint Christopher, but his head was in shadows. He was mostly a wall of checkers. I remembered playing checkers with Aunt Tifi. She had let me win until I was old enough to notice. I had protested that I wanted a fair game.

The distant bang of a door opened and closed. Dust wafted into my eye from some vault above, and I batted at my lashes to get it out. As I sat up, I saw Aunt Tifi standing beneath the saint.

I could hear the smile in her voice. "You thought I wouldn't make it, didn't you?"

"Aunt Tifi? Where have you been?" I stumbled toward the mural and banged my shin on the end of the pew.

She held out her arms and I limped forward to embrace her. "Where. . . ?"

"*Shhhh.*" She held a finger up to my lips. "The nuns are sleeping."

I'd forgotten I was a whole head taller than she. Tonight, we almost matched heights. Or, rather, her turban came to the level of my eyebrows. She was wrapped in a smock of purples and blacks. When she tilted the matching turban back to peer up at my face, she had to reach back to support it.

"I couldn't come 'til now." She stepped back and

tightened the knot atop her head.

"Why not?"

"I was playing hide and seek. Isn't the honey marvelous?" She shimmied her shoulders.

"Hide and seek? With whom?"

"Funny game. We learn how to play it as a child. We know that when you hide, you hide. When you seek, you seek. As we get older, we start hiding all the time. We hide behind makeup, clothes. We hide in fancy houses and cars and behind titles. And when we seek, we forget we can't be hiding to find."

"Aunt Tifi, it's late, I'm tired, and I have no idea what you're saying except that it has nothing to do with my questions."

"Oh, but it does. It always has. You just expect certain answers, so you don't hear the ones you're given." Her eyes sparkled. She blew a kiss to Saint Christopher and shook her head at me.

I sat back down on the pew. "What aren't you telling me?"

She joined me. "No, no. The question is what *am* I telling you?" She leaned over and placed her hands on my shoulders to whisper in my ear. At first, I closed my eyes against her words. Then I let myself breathe them in. They tasted sweet, after all.

When I opened my eyes, Aunt Tifi had turned into a nun with a very large nose.

CHAPTER 42

I looked around me. Altar, ceiling, pew—and, yes, the black habit of a nun.

I straightened. It was still dark, but the stained-glass windows were starting to warm with color. I looked at the nun who stood over me, her hand on my shoulder.

I asked, "Is it morning?"

She tilted her head in question.

"Jour?" I asked, pointing at the windows.

She nodded and held a finger to her lips.

I stood up and whispered *"Je désolée."* I pointed to the bench where Aunt Tifi had been sitting in my dream.

The nun smiled and shook her head. She held her hand to her heart and then to her lips. I gathered she was under some vow of silence. I nodded and moved away. When I reached the door, I glanced back to see her kneeling at the altar, no sign of Tifi anywhere.

❖

Outside, dawn was on its way. The silent square slept in lavender shadow. The tops of the buildings watched, still dull with night.

My body and mind were half asleep. I went around the back of the church and found myself in a tiny street wedged between medieval buildings. I followed the steep, cobblestone gradient. After the equivalent of a block, the buildings simply ended in countryside.

The cobblestone blended into a gravelly dirt path that wound past chicken coops and sheds to the edge of a vineyard. An ancient man in slippers and robe was scattering vegetable ends at hens. Their eager feathers formed an almost perfect circle around the scraps. The man nodded at me and then shuffled into a doorless barn. Beneath it, a low and slow brook stood almost still along the bottom of a gully.

And just beyond, perpendicular to the brook, stretched the unmistakable double line of plane trees. Here was the village's northernmost bend of canal. The head of the snaking water joined to the rest of the body with a canal bridge.

Chance had told me about places along the canal where Pierre had built water bridges that allowed the canal to continue over small valleys or ravines. It must be an odd sight to stand below such a bridge and see a barge travel above you. This water bridge was held up by a single arch spanning the brook below.

I picked my way along a path until it came to the level of the canal. I walked to the middle of the bridge's equivalent of a sidewalk. Turning slowly, I took in the gentle curve of trees winding out of sight, the jasmine and thyme, the church tower I had just come from. As I watched, the first rays of sun lifted over the town's tile roofs.

I sat down on the edge of the bridge's walk, my back to the water, my legs dangling over the stream below. The sun climbed. Aunt Tifi's dream words hovered in my head like the pollen on the water. I let my legs hang still.

Now fully bathed in sunlight, I slipped up my right pant leg and examined my shin. A fine, darkening bruise was beginning to spread below my knee. Just where I would have bumped into the pew if I had risen to greet my aunt.

If it hadn't been a dream.

CHAPTER 43

The bees were awake and lively. The sunny air was filled with the gentle scent of smoke, wax, and sweetness.

I checked all of my netting and nodded. "Ready."

Gilbert handed me the smoker. "When they think the forest burns, they eat. They fill their stomachs to save the honey. Doing all this, they ignore the people."

"They eat the honey? How do you get it then?" I asked.

Huguette squinted at me as if she was trying to read small print. "They put it back."

Gilbert had just lifted the lid off a hive. Inside was another shallow box with a screen across it and a few bees flitting atop the surface of a viscous substance.

Huguette elbowed me, and I puffed white smoke over the screen. "This is the top feeder. That is their food. The *sirop.*"

Gilbert picked up a kind of lever stick with a flat,

curved end. With one hand pressing down on the feeder, he held the lever in the other and gently pried the feeder from the hive body. "The parts are always sticking together," he told me. "But we must be careful to not make loud 'pop' sound. It scares them." He circled the box and loosened the other side.

I nodded, taking inventory of what I was feeling about all this. It was one thing to face a fear. It was quite another to try and enjoy it. I kept my breath regular as I felt sweat forming. All of my netting was secure. I puffed more smoke. I could do this.

In the box, only a few of the creatures shook themselves along the lines of the "files." Gilbert explained, "The smoke sends them back into frames."

"So they've started eating their honey?" I asked.

He smiled. *"Bon appetit."*

Ah yum, regurgitated honey.

Huguette waved at us. "Come. We don't keep the hive open too long."

Gilbert rolled his eyes and responded in French. He stood across the box from me. Bending over, he inserted his lever between the left end of the first frame closest to him and the frame next to it, moving his hand toward the center of the hive. He repeated this on the right end and then set the lever down. I continued to sweat. Could the bees smell it?

With both hands, Gilbert picked up the first frame by the end bars and lifted. Slowly, so slowly, he lifted the frame straight up and out of the hive. Sunlight shown over his shoulder and hit the rising sheet of waxen comb. The top third of the honeycomb was opaque and creamy white. This melded into a translucent strip and then thickened in the lower half to tan-topped cells. With many, many bees crawling all over them.

I stepped closer, trying to see through the netting of my veil. Gilbert continued to hold the frame aloft for me to see. I watched the glistening wings twitch and shift, circle and hop. Each perfect hexagon lined up, row upon row beneath them.

It was so fascinating, I forgot to pump the smoker.

Gripping the ends of the frame, Gilbert turned it vertically. Then he turned it toward himself and back away, like a page in a book. After scanning it, he finally turned it horizontally, taking a last look at the opposite side. He then, most carefully, set the frame down on the deck, leaning it up against the box. His movements were all as if underwater.

Huguette took the smoker from me as I stood riveted to the beautiful intricacies of something I had hated.

Gilbert examined the second frame in silence, returning it to the vacancy where the first had been. He continued to pry and lift, hold and turn, return. After the third frame, he said, "Always look close to not crush any bees. Especially not the queen. That would be tragedy."

Rows of bees lined up between the frames, all wiggly and glistening. "They are curious. Huguette. . . ."

She was already there with the smoker, sending a

curtain of white across the box. The bees retreated to eat.

I broke from my reverie. "Are you looking for mites?"

"Yes. And the queen."

"How can you find her in there with so many others?"

Gilbert looked back at the frame and smiled again. "She is sometimes like love. You may not see her, but you can see her effects. Look."

He held up a frame, and I came around behind him. He continued, "Get close, you can see eggs. The size of rice."

I looked over his shoulder, the sun behind us. Gilbert tilted the screen, and I bent over the hexagonal cells. He moved them closer to my netted face. I squinted and focused. I saw the larvae first— translucent C-shapes curled in the cells. And then I saw the eggs. Indeed the size of rice grains.

I smiled, "Love is home."

We spent the next couple of hours lifting, holding, shifting, and stacking. The sun warmed the entrances to the busy worlds and the three of us standing around them.

Finally, Gilbert stood with a frame to the light. "We are in the presence of royalty."

I carefully skirted the box at my feet and came around by his shoulder. He nodded to Huguette who came around his other side. She reached a finger to hover over a bee on the comb. There she was, larger and more elongated than the others. I was amazed she could be found amid this city of bees. I stood in admiration, one of her three, white-robed, royal court.

"Do you know they used to think the queen was a king?" Huguette asked.

"They?"

"Beekeepers," Gilbert answered. "Until the eighteenth century they think this. Even Virgil writes of king bees." He chuckled.

"Kings!" Huguette scoffed but kissed her husband, quick, through his netting.

Love was home, indeed.

CHAPTER 44

"Elliot."

"Mel? Well, well. How's France? Had frog legs yet?"

"No, but I did try the snails."

"I am impressed. Very brave of you."

"The snails were definitely the least impressive risk so far."

"What, have you taken to skydiving? SCUBA?"

"I'm keeping bees. And I'm calling to let you know I'm not just taking a vacation."

"As in. . . ."

"As in, I'm not coming back to work. I quit. I just extended my ticket."

"For how long?"

"It doesn't matter."

"Maybe it does. Maybe I could meet you in Paris. We could stay at that hotel near *Sainte-Chapelle*. I can write it off as a business trip. We'll 'research' all the old-school wine labels as inspiration for a new packaging campaign. Sounds pretty good, doesn't it?"

"All but the part where you come to Paris."

"That wasn't nice."

"You're right, but neither was your adventure with the secretary."

"Mel, I've apologized for that. It's over. I even hired that portly little grandmother to take her place, remember?"

"That's not exactly atonement."

"This is awfully short notice. You're not being very professional."

I laughed until I hung up on Mr. Once.

As I walked back along the tow path, I felt like I'd lost twenty pounds—of emotional weight. Before today, I might have softened at Mr. Once's offer of Paris. It was what we'd planned—the honeymoon I'd been dreaming of. But that was just the problem. We had both been better at dreaming than living.

I was ready to live.

I felt my father's presence as I walked back to the barge. For the first time—maybe in my life—I felt strong.

As I approached the lock house, Chance was emerging. When he saw me, he stopped. *"Bonjour,* Mel."

"Bonjour."

He gave half a smile. "I was sent to get you and

Gilbert. We are going to have a late lunch in the lock house garden. A celebration of the family business."

"The restaurant/distillery/*pension?*"

This time the smile was full. "Yes. And you are to thank for that."

"Oh, it was nothing. I can get Gilbert. I'm headed to the barge anyway."

"If you like."

"I like." The plane trees were dancing in the breeze. If I stood still any longer, it would definitely become awkward. I turned toward the lock. It waited, empty and deep.

I glanced at the mill. The building looked strong and ready for use. I imagined it with green shutters and red geraniums in window boxes, with white curtains flying out in the afternoon breeze. We could have weekend wine tastings, dinner theater. We could. . . .

We? I pivoted to look at *Der Honigschlecker* and realized I was thinking of myself now and in the future as being right here. It felt good. It felt like home.

On the barge, the bees were quiet. The hive entrances were empty. I felt sore from bending and lifting hives all morning. Good thing my aunt and uncle didn't have to do this all the time.

I called out, "Gilbert! We're wanted for lunch."

I heard a sound from the direction of the hives. I crossed the gangplank and heard another sound. I looked down and saw Gilbert half lying, half sitting on the deck against the prow edge, hand to his heart. He was taking ragged breaths.

"Gilbert!" I dropped down to my knees. "What's wrong?"

He looked at me, shaking his head.

I screamed across the canal, "Huguette! Chance! Help!" What was the word for help in French?

"Melissa." It was a whisper. He clenched my hand in a grip so tight my knuckles cracked.

"Yes?"

He spoke in French. I tried to hold on to the words, but I couldn't distinguish them. I was trying not to cry. "Gilbert, I don't understand."

He was fading but with a smile. I caught the words *"pas de plumes"* only because he kept repeating them as his eyes focused behind me. I turned to look and saw only the stained-glass Honeylicker Angel.

I leaned over to hug Gilbert, my tears falling onto his forehead as his breath left him. I heard a sound of someone running across gravel, and all of a sudden I couldn't breathe either.

I was four years old. Aunt Tifi was coming to visit. I kept looking out the window asking *when?* Mom kept saying *go play.* I ran outside past the rose bushes to the fence. I decided to find a special lookout. I found a gap in the fence and squeezed through. I crunched across the gravel drive in triumph—there sat a loamy tree stump. It gaped open, hollow and inviting. I climbed inside and disturbed a hive.

The bees were angry. I turned, raised an arm to my face, and screamed. They stung me in my armpit and along my side and face. The pain was sudden and terrible. I fell into the hive, consumed by a furious swarm.

I heard my father's voice calling me, but I couldn't even form his name.

CHAPTER 45

Someone was shaking me. I focused in hope, had Gilbert. . . ? No.

Chance's eyes were right across from mine. "Mel!"

My entire life filled the space between our faces. I had a hard time focusing on him. "It was my fault."

Chance's eyes were haunted and red. "It wasn't your fault."

I barely heard him. "The bees. When he came to get me, they stung him too. I held him so tight the bees crushed into him. He *was* allergic."

Chance let go of my shoulders and sat in a slouch of defeat. "My father wasn't stung."

"*My* father was. . . ."

"What are you talking about?"

"What does *"pas de plumes"* mean?"

"Mel this isn't. . . ."

"*Pas de plumes!* What does it mean?"

Chance looked at me in an odd blend of distance,

confusion, and pity. He finally answered. "No feathers."

I turned to look behind me. Of course he wouldn't be visible. But he was there. He was always there. I closed my eyes and saw him, my featherless angel. He lifted his arm to wave as his body dissolved into bees. They flew away and left me with the sound of flight. But it was flight of journey and destination, not fear.

The strength I'd felt earlier returned. Chance was right, even if he didn't know about my father. It wasn't my fault. It had never been my fault. I had allowed a lie to define me. I felt an instant ocean of compassion for the frightened little girl introduced to pain and loss, for the woman who had built a fortress to keep them out.

I smiled and reached for Gilbert's hand. He looked like he was sleeping. "Rest well, my friend."

Chance was still sitting, immobile, holding Gilbert's other hand. I reached for his shoulder, and he didn't move. He was staring at his father's face.

"I'm so sorry."

He said nothing. His face had gone rigid.

We sat, each of us holding the hand of a father we'd lost. The air was so still, all I could hear was the sound of Chance and I breathing.

The bees were silent.

She cradles bees in her open
fist and shakes them toward shore.
I am their queen she says. *You are
mine,* says the man at the prow.

They carry boxes of bees
from deck to forest,
chasing seasons of trees.
Their workers turn fir to honey
and dance back to lavender,
the sun as their guide.

You are my sun, says the woman,
standing in the man's arms.
And you are mine, he says as it sets.

Years ago they kissed *yes*
under an altar angel who licks
a finger just stuck in honey.
Tonight, the man asks again
for her hand, spins her out
and back in silence.

Dancing, the woman forgets
she was a girl afraid of bees, afraid
until she heard the hum of love
on the lobes of her ears. *Choose,*
he'd whispered, soft as water.

And so she'd chosen to break
open the sticky comb, to hold
the hand of the man who showed her
to salve her stings with the nectar
of those who could wound her.

Run a river of honey
between us to sweeten
every passage. . . .

PART FOUR

One month later . . .

CHAPTER 46

It is solstice, the day of honey harvest. The sky is still white when I wake. Water light dances on the roof of my room. I dress and head for the deck. I take a deep breath and stretch my arms to where the sun is rising. We have plenty to do on this longest day of the year.

From the barge, the mill looks like she, too, is rousing from sleep. A stack of lumber and torn soil shows that someone is shaking her awake.

To the left, a kitchen window at the restaurant is bright. Someone is readying dough. *Petits pâtés* are on the menu tonight.

And then the hives. I turn to face my new vocation. This is my version of Aunt Tifi's rose garden. The difference is: this garden takes to flight and relies on all other gardens. I have grown fascinated with their sweetness and light. I have finally begun to enjoy the bees.

For the first time in my life, I feel complete. Initially, this puzzled me. I had quit my job. I had walked away from my former fiancée. I had discovered Chance was engaged. I had just lost the man who most reminded me of my father.

But that's paradox. Loss turns to gain. Fear turns to love. And I see I can be in Love—the full-spectrum, capital-L Love. No person, place, or thing required. This has been a marvelous discovery.

I tiptoe into the galley to make coffee amid the mess Huguette and I left last night, preparing for the honey harvest. She appears in the doorway just as I plunge the coffee press. She gives me a look of begrudging approval, takes the bowls, and heads above deck. I follow her with the coffee.

We sit on the stern bench and each take the first sip of the day. The stained glass of the Honeylicker Angel fills with light.

I turn to Huguette, "What is the story of *Der Honigschlecker?*"

She takes another sip of coffee and looks at the angel. "You know of Gilbert's Father? Mattias was German."

"Yes. Gilbert told me about the *résistance* and the Strasbourg Cathedral."

"I know how he told that story. I will tell you the other half—Joan's half. Joan was Gilbert's mother. Joan wanted to become a *nonne*—how you say? Nun. She goes every day to the *cathédrale*. One evening, she walks through the *porte* and stops to look at it. It is a great thing, this door. Above it are Adam and Eve. Joan looks at Adam and Eve and thinks: *'Puhhh. They ruin everything. I can do better. I don't need to have a man.'*

"Inside, she sees Mattias arrive—who she does not know is Mattias, of course. She is watching this stranger pray as if his life depends on it. And suddenly she knows something. Adam had the entire creation. He had God to himself. And yet, he was lonely. He wanted more. So God made Eve. Joan sees Mattias, and she tries not to think of more. She closes her eyes, and when she opens them, she sees now there is another soldier praying with him. The two men kneel a long time. Finally, the second man leaves.

"Joan knows something new in her heart. She goes to sit next to Mattias. When he finishes prayers, he sees Joan, and he smiles as if he has known her all of his life. He asks her to marry him.

"The next week they leave Strasbourg and go to the *Bodensee*. You call it Lake Constance in English. I never know why these name changes. *Bodensee* is its name. It is at the bottom of Germany.

"They arrive late at night to the *Barockkirche Birnau am Bodensee*. This baroque church is pink and like a wedding cake. Inside lives the Honeylicker Angel."

I feel like a child learning the final clue on a treasure hunt. "So that's where he comes from."

"*Oc. Der Honigschlecker*. He watches over marriage, family, and everyone in love. And beneath his hive, Mattias and Joan marry. After, they go to Toulouse and discover the Canal du Midi. They fall in love with the canal. One morning, they are eating breakfast in a small *pension*. They talk about some day buying a *péniche*. A man at another table hears them. He says he has a *péniche* they might like. He takes them to the harbor to see it. There is *Der Honigschlecker*. Mattias and Joan, they think it is a dream or a joke. How is it possible? They tell the man about their wedding beneath the angel. The man smiles. He tells them they can have the boat if they promise they will keep the bees."

Huguette finishes the story as matter-of-factly as she would the dishes. Perhaps that is the way to respond to such blessings—as if they happen easily, daily, and in such magnitude.

I looked at the happy, little angel. Blaise had translated Proverbs 24:13 for me during our last lesson:

My child, eat honey, for it is good, and the honeycomb is sweet to the taste. In the same way, wisdom is sweet to your soul. If you find it, you will have a bright future, and your hopes will not be cut short.

CHAPTER 47

"*Bonjour,* Mom."

"Hello, dear. How are the French lessons?"

"Entertaining. Remember that medieval town I told you about, Carcassone? Blaise took me to Jacques and Michelle's to see the new baby and help with their honey harvest. I got to learn French and honey harvesting at the same time. I wish you could taste honey straight from the comb—straight from a hive warmed by the sun."

"Your aunt brought some home once. Not warm from the sun but such a pleasure. I kind of wondered if she'd show up there tonight."

"It would be her style; skip the funeral and come to the harvest party. That reminds me, I still need to pick the flowers. I'm in charge of decorations. The brothers wanted to do everything else."

"How are the brothers?"

"Busy. Gilbert surprised them with a sizeable

inheritance. Enough for the whole shebang—*pension* included."

"Hmm. I might just have to come and visit when it's finished. And these brothers, are either of them. . . . Are you. . . ?"

"Are we what, Mom?"

"You're going to make me ask, aren't you?"

"No, no. I'm as solo as the day is long."

"As long as it's not Elliot."

"No worries. Mr. Once is living up to his nickname."

Today, "brilliant" is a verb. As I'm returning from the phone booth, the morning sun "brilliants" through the leaves. The canal surface is series of glittering arcs formed by the flat wakes of slow barges. The air is fragrant with every flower the bees are pollinating. It is a fine day for a party.

When I approach the lock house, Mado is leaving it, a box under her arm. Blaise's voice, muffled, says goodbye from inside.

Mado waves at me. "Mel! *Moment."*

The young man operating the lock turns and sees us. He waves with one hand as the other finishes circling the rope around the pilings. We wave back. He is happy to now have a full-time job, and high season will keep him busy.

Mado has been in Paris since the funeral. We kiss

cheeks and she reaches for my arm. "You think maybe something wrong."

I'm not sure what this means.

The sluice closes. Roaring water drowns out conversation. Which is just as well. I still don't know what to say to her. We watch the rising water. The sunlight hits the frothing water and turns it to a glaring boil.

Mado is watching me. She says, "My sister visit me in Paris. Tell me about you and what she tell you. She was wrong."

She holds out the box. On it is the logo of Sophie's boutique in Carcassone. "It is for tonight. It is for. . . ." She searches for the words.

But I know before she tells me, and I try not to smile.

CHAPTER 48

In the kitchen, he is breaking open a head of garlic.
"Chance?"

He looks up.

"I want to apologize for something."

He raises an eyebrow.

"You remember the picnic at the *lac* right after I arrived?"

He continues to expose individual cloves. "Always."

"Just before we drove there, you took me to the boutique. Sophie told me something that was only partly true. But I believed all of it."

A look of suspicion passes over Chance's face. "It had maybe to do with Mado, yes?"

"Yes."

"It had maybe to do with the fact that we had been engaged?"

I smile. "To Sophie, you still were. So when . . .

236

when we were at the lake and you kissed me. . . ." I remembered the water running from us like it had from the emptying lock.

He whacks a clove of garlic with the side of his knife. "You could have asked if it was true."

"I could have done a great many things differently. But since I can't go back, I'm doing what I can now. Present tense."

He rubs the papery skins from the garlic. "That is good for you. Speaking of 'now,' how is the honey-making?"

I don't know what I expected—an embrace, the exchange of sweet nothings? The only sweetness in this conversation is the topic of honey, apparently. Fine. "It's going well. Your mother likes having someone to instruct."

He keeps up the rhythmic chopping, saying nothing.

"And I like the barge. I think it will be a great attraction for people staying at the *pension*. As long as they aren't afraid of the bees."

Chance shakes off a papery frill sticking to his thumb. "And if they are, you can tell them your story."

"Yes, I can tell them my story. My story without an ending." And with that, I leave.

CHAPTER 49

I am in the middle of the dining room when I hear him behind me. "Melissa," he says.

I turn around.

He leans into the doorframe and crosses his arms. "Mel. Your name is also short for 'melodramatic.' You find no endings when you walk out of the story."

I start to cross my own arms but realize I'm still holding Mado's box. "Walk out of what? I stayed on the barge with something I hated, something I was afraid of."

"Then why is it so hard for you to stay with something you might love?" He straightens and lets his arms fall to his sides.

"Something or someone?"

A slight smile teases the corner of his mouth. "You know what I think?"

"I'm not sure I want to."

"I think you have never forgiven me for dumping

chili powder in your hot chocolate. When I was fourteen."

"What?" I say it sharp and shrill. It sounds defensive and ridiculous. It is.

"It gives you a reason to be mad at me whenever you like. Not so fair. I don't have a similar reason."

"Are you asking for one?"

"No, I'm asking you to taste something. Wait here." He gestures toward a window table with the posture of a *garçon* and a half bow.

I hesitate and then take the offered seat facing the canal. As I wait, I try to reimagine being twelve the summer Chance visited. I think I hated that age, but I can't remember clearly.

Chance appears with a mug in his hand. "Hot cocoa for the *mademoiselle*. With chili."

I look at him, puzzled.

"Just a pinch, and sweetened with honey of course. I think I'll name it *Desire.*"

I accept the mug with both hands. He sits next to me. We both face the water. I am aware of the short distance between our hips, the rise and fall of his chest as he breathes.

Outside, another barge rises into the lock. I take a sip of the cocoa without hesitation. It is sweet and just spicy enough to make my tongue tingle.

He looks at me. Instead of asking what I think of it, he says, "Actually, I do have a reason to be mad at you."

"Oh?"

"Yes. At the lake, you kissed me back, and you thought I was with another woman. Very bad of you."

"Don't worry. I've beaten myself up about that already. I guess now we're even."

"OK, then. 'Clear slate'?"

"Clean slate." I try not to look at him. The chocolate drink is living up to its name.

Chance slaps his thighs and stands. "Well, back to work."

I am left with *Desire* and an unopened gift.

This is highly unsatisfactory. "Wait a minute, mister."

He is behind me, but I can hear him smile. He says nothing.

I set down my hot cocoa and stand. "What's this about not walking out?"

He's trying to look innocent. "I have much to do for tonight."

"So do I. It's a harvest party. Which usually involves a harvest."

"Then we're agreed, work first, play later."

"Play?"

He steps closer. *"Oui, mademoiselle."*

"I thought the French were known for mixing business and pleasure."

He is a breath away from me. "Ah, these stereotypes."

I can feel the hiss of his "s" on my lips. We are inches apart when he steps back and turns me toward the door. "Harvest time, honey."

My tongue tingles from more than the chili.

CHAPTER 50

I wonder if the bees know I'm about to take their honey?

I've set up the galley according to Huguette's directions. Newspapers cover the floor and counters. There are bread knifes to cut the combs. The extraction has to take place away from any bees—if they smell the honey, they'll swarm. And there will be plenty of honey to smell.

Work space prepared, I don my hat and jacket and return above deck. Huguette is waiting with the smoker. She points to me and then begins the smoke. "You start."

The air fills with the acrid scent of pine. I pull the lid off the nearest box. The bee beard around its entrance has shrunk to a goatee. The first frame slides out, heavy and dazzling, the hexagons brimming with gift.

They are giving me more than honey, these bees.

They have given me something to forgive. And as I do, I am able to forgive myself.

I feel light enough to take flight.

Morning blends into afternoon. Huguette and I spend the rest of the day back and forth between the deck and galley with the occasional irate bee and lots of sticky puddles. She gives me enough instruction to write a how-to book, and much of it I forget. But much of it becomes muscle memory. By early afternoon, Huguette has stopped talking, and we have enough honey to drizzle the town.

She is the first to call it a day. "Good work. We will take a rest before tonight."

Since Gilbert's death, Huguette has developed a respect for rest.

I nod. "I'm going to sit onshore."

On deck, I see the post has come. There is a letter from Aunt Tifi. I hold her missive like a talisman. It is dated several weeks ago from Tunisia. It looks like it traveled the entire way in a saddlebag.

I want to read it somewhere special. I jump over the gangplank to shore. The workers have already left the mill for the day. I slip past the garden and into the woods, walking parallel to the canal and emerging at my little spot on the bank.

The light is buttery soft and the air warm. I kick off my sandals, roll up the legs of my trousers, and sit near the edge of the grassy bank. I rest my ankles and feet in the green canal and pull out the letter. I remember a pink envelope not so long ago in a Chicago hospital bed.

The spidery script is crazily slanted and cragged, as if Aunt Tifi had been writing in a truck on pot-holed roads.

My dearest Melissa,

This letter might take a while to arrive. I'm writing on the back of a camel in the middle of the desert. Though I've grown enamored of these beasts, the process of dismounting (and mounting, for that matter) is completely inelegant. So I wait aloft for Luc to barter with a vendor for some figs.

I find it providentially amusing that I have fallen in love with another man with 'Luc' in his name. Make the most of second chances.

We are visiting Luc's home a few villages away. He is the son of French missionaries, a widower with three children I've yet to meet. And so, of course, I think of you. You have always been like a daughter to me.

I had a dream about you. I was telling you this story: when Luc's parents came to Tunis, they bought an ancient truck to help bring supplies wherever there were roads. One day, Luc and his parents were going to a larger market a few towns away. A local villager was beginning a long journey to the interior, and Luc's father offered him a ride. This villager was a very respectful and considerate man, and he knew the cab of the truck would be filled by Luc and his parents. The man accepted the offer only if he could ride in the back with his two, large suitcases.

As they pulled out of the village, Luc's family heard bumping and shuffling noises in the bed of the truck. Luc looked around—he was about eight at the time—and said, "Mon père! *He is standing up . . . standing up and holding his suitcases!"*

His father looked back, and sure enough, the man was standing with his legs planted wide, his large bags banging between his calves and the sides of the truck bed. Beads of sweat ran down his temples. The father stopped the truck and went outside to ask what the man was doing.

"Sir," the man said, "I do not want to make the load heavy for the truck. I am holding my bags to keep the journey light."

I have learned to set down a great number of burdens, my dear. I hope you have too.

The writing changed to her normal cursive:

Now I write you from a campfire. We are under magnificent skies and my fingers are sticky with figs and honey sucked from the comb.

I'm not going to read what I've already written— partly because the flame light is dim, and partly because I rarely go back, as you know.

I wonder if you are learning any French? I have a feeling you are. My nephews are both good teachers. If you haven't already, ask one of them to teach you.

The French are a sensory people. I sometimes wonder if they have a beautiful, collective case of synesthesia. Look up the verb sentir, and you'll see what I mean.

Did you enjoy the books I sent you? The Little Prince, especially, is such a treasure of a book. One of my favorite ideas of Saint-Exupery's is that we can only see the essentials with our hearts.

Open the eyes of your heart, my dear.

Love always,

Your Tifi

CHAPTER 51

The flowers are saturated in late afternoon light. I tuck Tifi's letter in my pocket and head for the field. Like the bees, I want the best.

I grab a large basket and shears from the barge deck and wait at the lock again. A young American couple in a small white boat are descending—the last passage of the day. They are laughing and kissing between coils of rope. Even when they move apart, their bodies curve in echoes of the other, as if waiting to reconnect.

They wave and say *bonjour*. I do the same. The woman pulls on the man's sleeve and points to the restaurant where the band is setting up. "Look, they must be having a party."

The couple's barge passes through the lock, the bridge comes together. I cross and walk down the path toward the field. When I get to the spot I stood my first morning in France, I stop.

"Thank you," I tell him.

I snap off a stem of lavender, tickle the tiny flowers, and wave them in front of my nose.

Sentir. To smell and to feel. I could add: to hear, to taste, to see. And those are only the natural senses.

I return to the barge with a basketful of flowers and not much time to shower and dress. But I have one thing more to do.

"Huguette?"

She is on her way up the wheelhouse. Impatient, she asks, "What?"

"I have something for you. Wait on deck, I'll bring it up."

I run to my room and return with the present. She is wearing a red dress with a sweetheart neckline and a full skirt that sways in the evening breeze. She has curled her short hair close in a style from half a century ago. There is a bit of romance in her after all. She doesn't ask what I think, but I can tell she wants to know.

"You look wonderful. Happy anniversary. And happy harvest."

She accepts the thin box and opens it. Inside is a scarf I found at an antique store in Carcassone. It is 1920s black burnout velvet with a slinky fringe. It dates from the same decade as the barge. The design is of wings. She lifts it from the box and gently drapes it around her shoulders. The fringe swirls as she reaches forward.

She gives me a quick hug—a first. And without a word, she leaves the barge. From Huguette, this silent gratitude speaks the loudest.

It is a day of gifts. I am curious what Mado gave me. I postpone the surprise until I've showered. I set the box on my bed, slip off the ribbon, and lift the lid. Inside is the dress from Sophie's shop window. I lift it out by its thin straps and hold it to my body. It *is* the color of acacia honey. It feels like a river on my skin. I gently slip into it and wish for a full length mirror. Even without seeing, I know it is perfect.

When I arrive at the restaurant, the jazz band has just begun. I set the basket of lavender and daisies on a table. Mado greets me with a wink and runs a finger along a side seam of my new dress. *"Oui.* I thought so. Perfect. She points to the flowers. "I get something for them." She returns with a tray of glasses.

Together, we measure handfuls of long lavender stems like dry spaghetti, tie them with daisies, and set them in highball glasses on each table. I strew the remaining daisies over the grass between the picnic blankets where two girls are making snow angels without snow. I toss a handful of daisies over them, and they screech in joy and competition to catch them.

Guests begin arriving. I duck inside to check on the brothers. Blaise is bartender. Chance is in charge of the kitchen.

"Everything OK in here?" I ask.

"It will be," Chance answers. Blaise is arguing with a waiter over a bottle.

"Will be? Can I help?" I peek behind him at the half-dozen people bumping into each other in the kitchen.

"You can help by dancing with me after. . . ."

Blaise zooms past, sees me, and interrupts, "Did you tell her?"

Chance rolls his eyes and mumbles something I can't hear. Blaise grins. "Why not now? Mel. . . ."

This time Chance interrupts. "Fine. Blaise and I were talking. We think it's time *Der Honigschlecker* moved again. Like she used to."

A dish crashes to the floor in the kitchen. Blaise yells *merde!* and bolts away.

I am surprised to feel jealous of the barge. The thought of it being taken away from me leaves me feeling dimmed.

Chance continues. "In the spring, she could follow the blooming flowers like she did when Joan and Mattias ran her. Maybe she can even take guests from the *pension.*"

"Won't you and Blaise be busy with everything here?"

"Well, I was thinking you would go."

My heart leaps up. "And what if I don't know how to pilot a barge?"

"Then I would offer my services. Maybe I could convince Huguette to help out here in the kitchen while I am away—if it is for a special reason."

250

"What special reason?" I can feel the scent of lemon zest on his knuckles.

He smiles and starts to speak, but another, louder crash sounds from the kitchen, and Blaise hails his brother.

Still smiling, Chance says, *"moment,"* and ducks back into the kitchen.

Blaise notices me again and smiles. "Melissa, you look *superbe*. Can you get something on the barge? We need another bottle of mead for the toast. It is in the room of *mon père*. In the chest."

"Certainly."

On the terrace, a few more families have arrived. I notice one right away. "Michelle!"

She smiles and lifts her little boy. "Gilbert is very much awake, tonight."

For a second, I think of his namesake. This new Gilbert regards me with wide eyes. I tell Michelle, "He looks like he knows what I'm thinking."

She laughs. "Oh, but he does. He is very smart, this one. Jacques!" She calls her husband and asks him to get a blanket from their car. I realize she was speaking French, and I understood.

I look at Gilbert. "Just you wait. This language business is quite a journey."

Michelle laughs and shifts him in her arms. "Especially when we use words."

The last rays of sunlight are filtering across the canal and spotlighting the guests. I disappear behind the hedges and descend into the courtyard.

Some of the children are running back and forth across the lock bridge. The lock is closed for the night, and barges have lined up on either side to wait till morning. I am surprised to see the American couple moored directly across from *Der Honigschlecker*. They are dancing to the music.

I slip below deck into my aunt's room. In the chest are several bottles of mead. I recognize the *Hydromel* and lift one out.

Above deck, the sun is at an angle that takes your breath away. It is cradled in the "Y" of a plane tree, as if in a slingshot aimed directly through the Honeylicker Angel in his bright, glass home. I close my eyes. Instead of darkness, the world beneath my eyelids is a glowing bowl of honey. I practice seeing with the eyes of my heart.

As I do, a face appears—a different face than the one I once saw. He is looking straight at me. When I open my eyes, he is still there. I blink.

He takes the honey wine from me and then takes a kiss. I give him one back.

Well, more than one.

O taste and see. . . .

EPILOGUE

The following spring . . .

Smoke and bees.

That pairing has become a comfort, familiar as old friends. They mingle with a breeze from the east. Today, we will reach the Sea. I will see sun on the water and taste the salt on my skin after a brisk swim.

I am thinking of this as I lift the lid, gloveless, from a hive. I accidentally grab a bee. The sting is fast and hard. I hold my breath and hand tight.

I let go of both and examine the almost invisible dot. I lick the sting. As my tongue hits skin, I turn the salve into a kiss.

GRATITUDE

This book was born and raised in houses around the world. Thanks to these friends and their homes:

Ralph & Catherine (and your inspiring relatives) of Huémoz, Switzerland and Llançà, Spain

Abby & Tom of Billings, Montana

Mark & Krissy of Medford, Oregon

Gary & Nancy of Jacksonville, Oregon

L'Abri & the attic of Les Sapins, Switzerland

Sarah & Roarke of the Applegate, Oregon

Cathy & Paul of Ashland, Oregon

Ben & Rebecca (once also of) Kanat Tabla, Saipan, Northern Mariana Islands

The Elkins of "Elkinsville," Jacksonville, Oregon

And a mighty thanks to Nathan Bransford, Julie Brooks Barbour, Joe Chermesino, Elizabeth Henke, Janet Keating, Hayley Mete, and the McCall's for working with me on *The Honeylicker Angel*.